BOUND to DECEPTION

USA Today Bestselling Author
J.L. BECK
New York Times Bestselling Author
MONICA CORWIN

Copyright © 2021 by Bleeding Heart Press

www.bleedingheartpress.com

Cover design by C. Hallman

Cover image taken by Wander Aguiar

All rights reserved.

No part of this book may be reproduced in any form or by any electronic or mechanical means, including information storage and retrieval systems, without written permission from the author, except for the use of brief quotations in a book review.

1

CILLA

*I*t's difficult to apply mascara when your hand is shaking harder than a gambler waiting for his next win. Hell, it's difficult to do anything when you know this is the night you're going to die. I blink away the tears threatening to ruin my makeup and take a few shallow breaths so I don't fog up the mirror two inches in front of my face.

A deep baritone voice calls from outside the dressing room. "Cilla, babe, get out here. You're late." *Shit.* I thought I had more time to talk myself into this.

I curse again and press my forehead to the cold glass. Something to ground me. Anything. Then I swallow all the self-hatred, the noise in my head, everything telling me I'm going to fail, and shove it deep. It won't help me get through the night unscathed, but at least I can go out with some fucking dignity.

I quickly finish my makeup, stash my kit in my locker, and jam my feet into the six-inch platform heels that will have my toes blistered by the end of the night.

Frankie is standing outside the door, staring pointedly at his watch. "Finally finished, princess? We gotta get to the bar. The crowd is already growing."

I wave him off, marching past him toward the lounge area. He cuts me off before I can head into the VIP section. "You were late. The quota is full for VIPs. You're at the bar to pick up stragglers."

It's fine. I lie to myself like I always do as I ramp up my fake-ass smile, turn, and head toward the bar rail. The crowd at the bar is thin, like usual, so this will be my punishment for being late. But it doesn't matter. I have business to attend to here first.

I skirt the end of the rail and sidle up to a man in his thirties parked on a barstool. By the size of the mess around him, he's been waiting a while.

"Hey, handsome." I give him a smile I don't feel.

He drops his gaze to my feet and gives me a slow perusal until he reaches my breasts. "Hey."

I barely keep from rolling my eyes. "Looking for a date tonight?"

He shrugs. "Could be. How much we talkin' here?"

I reach in front of him, so I can curl around his upper arm, pressing my breasts into his bicep. "Oh, I don't know. A handsome fellow like you? I can probably give you a discount."

As he shifts, he slides his hand over mine, shoving a tiny plastic-wrapped package under my fingers. The move is so smooth that I understand why Essex is said to be the best at drops.

He gives me another long look and pats the back of my hand, making me clench the tiny packet. "Nah, babe, I don't think I can afford you tonight. But thanks."

I shrug softly like it's his loss and turn. I don't make it a step before his hand lands on my ass with a loud crack. A sharp pain radiates from the contact, but I clench my jaw and continue walking away.

When I return to the other end of the bar, I keep my hand closed around my prize and do not rub the sore spot on my ass from the slap.

One part of my plan is in motion. Now I just need the other part.

Ivan.

One of the most dangerous men in the city. And the man who is likely going to kill me before the night is over. I keep my smile wide even as a chill races down my spine. How did I get myself into this mess?

The bartender slides a glass of soda water with lime in front of me. I give him a grateful nod and spin to survey the VIP section. Ivan always ends up there when he comes in. I need to be waiting so he doesn't pick up another girl or, hell, just walk through and not stay.

I stare around, hoping to catch a glimpse of his usual black-on-black suit or the black ink scrawled up his long neck and over his graceful fingers. Not that I've been staring at him too often. Only enough to be able to recognize him quickly.

I slide down the bar to perch on a stool, glad Frankie is distracted with some of the new girls at the far end of the VIP section. He'd be pissed if he caught me sitting.

The music changes, and I keep my eyes on the VIP section and down the bar in case he enters that way. Usually, he comes from the back, but I want to be prepared either way.

The air in the club changes, and it's almost like the building itself is holding its breath. I swallow the sudden knot in my throat and watch for him.

As usual, he enters from the back of the VIP section. Frankie and a couple of the girls lock eyes on him, but Ivan keeps his gaze forward. At least he looks relaxed tonight. Some nights, he comes in wired, almost looking for a fight.

Frankie moves from the corner of my eye, shoving one of the new girls after Ivan.

Oh, hell no. This one is mine. At least for tonight.

I race up the short steps and cut her off. "You don't want to do that, honey."

I grab her arms like I just steadied her from a fall. "Seriously. Let me take this one. Go back to Frankie. Let him start you on someone a little less…brutal."

Her eyes widen, and then she spins and practically races back to Frankie and the other clustered girls.

I don't wait and give Frankie a chance to stop me. I spin and rush after Ivan as quickly as possible in six-inch heels. He throws his long frame into a booth, and I drop myself dead center on his lap. "Hey, gorgeous, looking for a date?"

He drops his dark gaze to mine. There's a hardness there. A steel that threatens to bend me to his will with just a look. My blond hair has tumbled over my shoulders and pools between us, keeping me from getting a better look at him up close. "Who are you?"

His voice is deep, dredged in darkness, and dare I say it…*desire*. Shit. I hadn't expected to actually react to him. It's been a long time since my body awoke for a John.

I swallow and smile. Not my fake megawatt smile with teeth. Just a wry twist of my lips, barely a smile. "Priscilla."

"Why are you sitting on me, Priscilla?" His tone is sharp enough to draw blood.

Luckily for me, I grew up with men like him. Crazy bastards who will do anything to get ahead. I don't even flinch.

"You looked a little lonely. Thought I'd come offer you my company. Would you like a drink? I'd be happy to get us both one."

I teeter on his legs, and he spreads his solid thighs to give me more real estate. His fingers dig into my spine, holding me so I don't fall. One of his hands comes up to catch my chin so he can look at me, and I spot black fingernail polish on his pinky. Strange. "Fine. Make it quick. I've got shit to do tonight."

I give him a wink, hop off his lap, and head toward the bar. The girl I'd cut off is waiting there with a pout. "Frankie says you just screwed me over by taking that guy. That he's a big tipper."

I signal the bartender, and he spots Ivan over my shoulder. While he makes the drinks, I turn to face the new girl. "What's your name?"

"Amanda." She crosses her arms under her breasts to give her waif-thin frame some bulk.

It takes a lot more than a hundred-pound kid to rattle me. "Look. He is a big tipper, but he likes to do things that would take your pretty fair skin a lot longer to recover from."

Her eyes go wide, and she drops her gaze to the tiny, faded pucker scars up and down my right bicep. I don't say a word and let her draw her own conclusions.

"What made those marks?"

The bartender sets our drinks in front of me, and I pull them close. "Cigarettes, honey. Those are burns from cigarettes."

She leans in and whispers, "Did he do that to you? What else did he do? Why didn't you call the police?"

I sigh and give her a look she hopefully takes as me calling her stupid without calling her stupid. "You don't call the cops around here. That's just not how it works."

"But they said everyone here works for themselves. That everyone is happy to be here."

I shrug. "We are all here of our own free will, but see if you can get a cop out here, especially for one of Doubeck's crew."

This time I've finally gotten to her. She recognizes the name. As anyone from around here would. The color drains from her face, and she races around me, down the hallway back to the dressing room. I chuckle. She wouldn't have made it in this life anyway.

Now that the coast is clear, I maneuver the drinks and slip the tiny packet of drugs Essex gave me into the double shot of vodka.

Then I give it a bit of a swirl and clutch the glasses close to my chest so he has a reason to look. I need him on the line before I reel him in.

I head back to the VIP area and slide into the empty spot he left at the edge of the booth for me.

He stares down at my cleavage or the drinks; either way, he's looking. "What are you drinking?"

I peek at the clear liquid in the glass. "Vodka, same as you, I think."

I never drink when I'm working, but tonight is an exception. It might make certain things easier to take, but tonight, I don't want to be clear-headed. At least if half of what they say about Ivan is true.

He grabs his glass and holds it in his hand as his arms spread across the back of the booth. The motion strains the seams of his black suit. He's handsome in an edgy, I'll fuck you so hard you'll be sore, kind of way. Too bad he's going to murder me soon.

I hold my glass up. "Cheers?"

His eyes narrow, and he scoots closer to me in the booth. The motion is silent. Not even the leather of the seat creaks as he moves. I catch the scent of him, something smoky and dark. It should disgust me. Turn me off, knowing how the night is about to go, but I can't seem to make my brain hate him. Hell, he's not the one sitting here trying to drug me. Whatever happens tonight, I'll have brought on myself.

"You look nervous. Do I make you nervous..." He pauses. "Priscilla, was it?"

I clutch my drink in both hands and nod. "You can call me Cilla if you want."

"Ivan."

I nod and don't explain how all the girls know the entire Doubeck family lineup. Landing one for the night is bragging rights for a while. Especially now with so many seemingly off the market.

"Well, Cilla." He shifts his legs until his thigh presses against the outside of mine. "Do you want to go somewhere a bit more private with me?"

I swallow, my gut churning. Shit. This is it. I thought I was prepared. I thought I was ready. Now I feel like I'm going to puke and run away at the same time.

No. I have to do this. One way or the other.

If Ivan kills me...I'm free.

If I manage to drug him...and survive...my father will let me go.

No more late-night visits to his drunk friends. No more using me to seduce unsuspecting clients.

So...there's only one way forward. I give him another smile. My real one and nod. "Let's go."

2

IVAN

The little prostitute, half my size, tried to drug me. From the second she threw herself on my lap, I smelled bullshit in the air. But she's cute with her long blond hair, and I caught a hint of garter under the edge of her black dress. So instead of pulling out my gun and putting a bullet in her temple, I let her play things out.

My paranoid nature means I never take drinks from strangers. In case I find myself in a situation where I might have to drink something, I always wear a thin layer of drug-detecting nail polish on my pinky finger. Andrea gives me shit about it, but after tonight, she's never going to be able to laugh at me again.

I barely inserted my finger into the drink, and the polish lit up pink. Kai will get pissed at me if I shoot her in our casino, so I'll take her somewhere private and handle things from there.

She slides out of the booth and wobbles on her ridiculous shoes. No way in hell she'd be able to run in those if she needed to. I snag her drink and mine off the table and tip my head toward the exit.

We head toward the elevator, and she stops, frozen, staring at the chrome doors.

I crowd her on the other side. "Are you going to push the button?"

She shakes herself and rushes over to jab the up arrow. "Sorry, got distracted for a moment."

As we step inside and the doors whoosh shut, I can't resist the urge to fuck with her a little bit. "You didn't name your price."

She turns to look up at my face. Damn, she has to be at least a foot shorter than me. Gun it is, then. Strangling her would be uncomfortable.

"Oh uh…I just liked the way you looked. On the house tonight."

I chuckle darkly as the elevator stops. "Your house is my house, as you well know."

Instead of waiting for her, I head toward the suite, giving her one last chance to reconsider. If she walks away now, I'll tamp down the urge to chase her. Hell, I might not even hunt her down in the future.

As I expect, she follows me toward the door of my suite. I jostle the glasses, keeping the drugged one in the front, and swipe the key card to enter the room.

Once inside, the heavy door slams shut, and I lock it and latch it behind her.

She watches, then turns to face the dimly lit room. It's sparse. Unlike my family, I don't need much. A bed, a bar, a closet, and a bathroom, are about it.

I watch her closely as she surveys my suite, her gaze lands on a pile of weapons stacked neatly on a side table. "That is a lot of knives."

Slowly, I inch closer to her. "The better to cut you with, my dear."

She spins to face me, no doubt realizing she left a predator behind her. "Ha ha, very funny."

I don't laugh and thrust the drink toward her. "Cheers."

She takes it and holds it up between us. I clink mine against hers, lock our gazes, and throw the two shots of vodka back like it's water.

When she does the same, I take both glasses and sit them on the bar. A warm hand touches my back, so warm I can feel it through my suit jacket.

"Why don't you take this off, hmm...get comfortable?"

I shrug out of it without facing her and drape it over my weapon pile. There are enough knives on me that I'll be fine if she decides to kill me when her plan fails.

Finally, when I know I won't lash out, following the dark thoughts jabbering through my head telling me to do unspeakable things to her, I turn. She's bathed in the dim light, and her tan skin glows. The dress cups her wide hips and full breasts so well I can't help but look.

She shifts to catch the light off her cleavage. "See something you like?"

I do a quick check to make sure she didn't drug me after all. It's not like me to be attracted to anyone. A good fuck is fine, but I don't make a habit of sitting around and checking put women. They are usually too stupid, and I get turned off when they open their mouths. For some reason, I'm not feeling that with Cilla.

"All right, *Malyshka*, you have my attention. What's your plan now?"

She saunters closer and grabs my dress shirt right above my belt. "The plan is to get you naked as quickly as possible, so I can have my way with you."

I stare down into her soft brown eyes and try to figure out where she is going with this. If her plan was to drug me to seduce me, then it's a pretty good way to fucking piss me off instead. "And what does that entail?"

She huffs with a soft laugh. "You want me to spell it out step by step."

I shrug and undo the buttons at the top of my shirt while she works the bottom. "If you like."

Her mouth turns down into a grim line for a heartbeat, then tips back up at the edges. "Well, first, I want to get you out of these clothes. Then...maybe we can move over to the bed. Although, it looks like we might have to move your machete out of the way to use it."

I nod solemnly. "Safety first, yes?"

She jolts and blinks. "Was that a joke?"

I give her nothing as I slide the shirt off my shoulders and toss it onto my jacket. The tie I had on goes with it. Her hands fly up to my belt buckle, and I grab her wrists. "What else do you have planned?"

I love the slight tremor of fear she gives me. Her entire body quakes with just this tiny touch. What would she do if I laid her facedown over the end of my bed and ate her pussy until she screamed? Her soft, throaty voice would sound so good screaming for me.

Her hands flutter against my buckle, and I release her to continue her work. My cock is already hard at what I'm imagining doing to her. What could she be thinking about?

After she releases my belt and pulls it out of my pants, she meets my eyes again. "You want the gory details or the headlines?"

"Details."

"Mmm...you seem like that kind of guy. Well, once we are both naked and safely on the bed, I plan to press my wet pussy down over your rock-hard dick and ride you like a goddamn pony."

I picture this situation in my mind and don't hate it. Well, I wouldn't if she hadn't tried to drug me. The drugs should be kicking in at any moment. The nail polish on my finger lit up bright, so she put a lot in that drink.

She opens my pants, and I allow her to slide her hand in to rub over my erection. "Oh, I see we are already making progress."

Her eyes have gone a little glassy, and she pumps her hand down my length harder. "You feel so warm and good."

I continue to monitor her. She doesn't seem to be sleepy or falling over. Then she bites her bottom lip and closes her eyes as she strokes me over my boxer briefs.

Oh. She tried to drug me with some kind of aphrodisiac. It makes sense.

She rubs me harder, and I close all the distance between us. "Baby. Why don't you take your clothes off too?"

Her eyes fly open, and she nods. "Yes, this dress is so itchy and hot. I want it off. Get it off me now, please."

I turn her and tug the zipper so she can strip the sequined scrap off her body and leave it puddled on the floor.

The soft curve of her spine tempts me, and I don't try to resist as I trail my index finger down the length of her body until I reach her ass.

Her lingerie is black lace, a full garter belt, and everything. She certainly came to make an impression. "What now, *Malyshka*?"

She starts for the bed and then stops in the middle of the room. I catch the edge of a muffled curse. Then she spins to face me, a fake smile spreading her mouth wide. "You know, I should go. This was probably a dumb idea. I'll get fired…"

I watch her as she snags her dress off the floor and rushes to the door. There's no way out now. She fumbles with the latch and the lock, managing to get the latch off before I snag her around the waist and rub my erection against her firm, round ass.

She braces her hands flat on the door and moans.

The sound of it sears me, but I won't do much more than this. At some point, when the drugs have fully taken hold of her, she'll beg for mercy.

Then learn...I don't have it in me.

"Back to the bed, baby. You were telling me what you were going to do to me."

She cuts off a strangled sound and turns to look at me. Her eyes are full-on hazy now, she's listing to the side, but her nipples are puckered, begging for my teeth.

Just a taste. A tiny one. I lean in and capture the stiff peak of her right nipple through the lace. She arches into me and clutches my head tighter to her chest. I scratch my stubble over the upper curve of her breast as I move to the other side and do the same.

This time she huffs out an impatient breath. "I need you inside me. Right now."

I take a moment to drag the honeycomb scent of her into my lungs. Let it fill me up because this is all I'll allow myself of her. I straighten and tug her toward the bed. "Sit, please, get comfortable. I'm not going to fuck you against the suite door. This time at least."

A pink flush hits her cheeks and spreads down her neck over the tan top of her tits. She's straining against the lace, panting, as the drugs take hold of her body and turn it against her.

"Bed," she whispers. "Right."

I kneel slowly and sit her down, and unbuckle the straps of her heels. Each of her toes is painted a soft pastel sort of pink. Without her shoes, her feet don't even touch the floor from the edge of my bed. She's so tiny. How would she even be able to take me? I'd break her open and enjoy it.

She wiggles her toes and arches her back. "That's better, thank you."

"Do you want another drink?"

"Water, please."

I leave her on the bed and cross the room to grab a couple of bottles of water out of the mini refrigerator. She's kneading the covers with her hands and rocking forward when I return. I hold the bottle out to her, and she takes it but runs it over her chest and down her belly instead of drinking it. The condensation leaves wet trails over her golden skin.

I sit beside her on the bed, not looking at her, and crack the top of my water. "You know, the first rule of drugging someone should be ensuring you get the fucking drugs in their body instead of your own."

3

CILLA

*E*ven as I wobble to my feet and try to make it to the door, I know my attempt at an escape will be useless. I can't even walk straight; my entire body feels like it's on fire from the inside out. My pussy keeps clenching on nothing, begging to be filled.

The bastard must have switched the glasses when we came upstairs. I'd been too nervous, too scared of him noticing the drugs that I swallowed it all down. The dosage was for a fully grown man of his height and weight. Not me...someone half his size.

I fumble with the lock on the door, the latch still open from our original grapple. My hand slides uselessly off it as a spasm rocks me. It's not an orgasm, and it's only the beginning.

It helps that I have a tolerance for this particular drug. It's been a while since I've taken it. Never of my own free will. Fuck. Is this a setup? Did my father give me the drugs knowing how it would turn out since I refused to be his guinea pig any longer?

Hands clamp around my hips, and I moan at the contact. He

easily lifts me off my feet and carries me back to the bed. Tears leak from my eyes, and I angrily swipe them away. "Let me go."

He chuckles a deep dark rumble that thrums my nerve endings. "Let me go," he mocks. "I'm not the one who did this to you, *Malyshka*. You did this to yourself."

He places one big hand over my bare stomach to hold me on the bed. Is he going to fuck me? It would be rough and brutal, and maybe exactly what I need. Wasn't that the plan? Fuck him into submission...

I can't pretend I'm even remotely more than a pawn in my boss's plans. Not anymore. Not after this fuck up. If Ivan doesn't kill me, my boss will.

"Please," I whimper. I hate the fucking noise coming out of my mouth right now.

He roughly strips my stockings off, ripping them in the process, and I writhe for it. Needing more of the elastic cutting into my skin, his rough fingers leaving bruises on my belly. All of it. Any of it. It's the sensation I need most of all.

His gaze is heavy as he strips my stockings off my feet and then uses one of them to tie my wrists to the heavy wood headboard. My legs are free, but he takes the other stocking and ties one ankle to the end of the bed. Then he exits and returns and uses his tie to take care of my other ankle, leaving me spread wide open for him. At least he hadn't taken my panties off yet. He hasn't witnessed how shamefully sopping wet I am right now.

"Is this how you pictured the night going, *Malyshka*? You tied to my bed, begging me to take you?" His voice reaches into me, stoking the fire. I drop my gaze to his open pants and spot the outline of his hard cock bulging against the open zipper. He's still hard, and he was big, one of the biggest dicks I've ever felt in my life, and I've touched many.

I drop my head back again to stare at the ceiling. A pulse of arousal scorches me, and I try to ride it out. It's the only thing to do if I can't have actual sex.

"What do you want?" I grit out. "I'll fuck you...I'll make you come harder than you ever have in your life."

He crawls up on the bed to brace his body on all fours over mine, not touching me at all. "I don't need you to get off. In fact, this display, you lying here like a cat in heat, is enough to take care of my own needs."

I whimper at the image of him thrusting up into his own hand, pumping thick ropes of cum down his shaft and onto his thickly muscled thighs.

He dips his head but still doesn't give me what I crave. "You like the idea of me stroking myself while I watch you. What other dirty thoughts are in that head of yours, hmmm?"

His eyes are dark in the dim room, his tattoos and scars stark against his skin. I can't keep my eyes off him. His pulse is jumping in his neck, telling me he's not as unaffected by me as he wishes.

"Is it because I'm a prostitute? Is that why you won't touch me?"

He scoffs and rolls easily off the side of the bed to stand at the end again. "I don't give a shit about what you choose to do for a living. I won't touch you, especially not with my cock, because you haven't earned it yet. You tried to drug me, and I assume when I was mindless with need, kill me?"

I shake my head frantically, lifting so my neck is aching at an angle. "No, I didn't plan to kill you."

His eyes narrow. "You didn't plan any of this, did you? You're just carrying out someone else's orders. So who sent you? Tell me, and I might give you some relief."

I whimper and drop my head down again. My pussy

clenches, and I try to shake it off, but I need some stimulation. I need to come so bad it hurts on the inside. "I don't know what the plan was. I just had to give you the drugs and do my job."

"Someone paid you to drug me and fuck me? To what end? Did you even consider that I'm a man with very fragile control? If these drugs had gotten into my system, I could have fucked you into the mattress until you were nothing more than a corpse."

Another whimper escapes as his weight comes up on the bed again. He grabs the panties at my hips and rips them away with one sharp swipe of a knife. The pull of the lace is enough to make my overheated body clench again.

He shifts, and when I open my eyes, he's standing over me. Standing on the bed, boots and all, between my spread thighs. He lifts one of his boots and presses the toe right over my clit.

I screech and arch up off the bed, fighting the bonds. "You gave me something, so I'll give you something. A little bit of relief, like I promised. But again, you haven't earned my cock. Not my mouth. My fingers. Nothing but my boot. So if you want it, take it."

It is awkward at first, me trying to get myself off on the tip of his boot, but it doesn't take long. I writhe my hips, arching against his foot until I get the friction I need. When I come, I see stars, and again my pussy clenches around nothing, shooting another wave of pain through me.

I don't think I'll last the night, but I assumed he'd just shoot me, not torture me to death. My skin is hot, and the bonds are cutting into my wrists and ankles. A gut-churning wave of nausea rolls through me as my humiliation follows.

I just rutted against his boot to fucking come, and I'd do it again.

As if sensing my thoughts, he lifts his shoe and kneels on the bed next to me. "Anything else you want to share? You want to earn some more relief, *Malyshka*?"

He adjusts his hard-on to sit more comfortably, then completely ignores it. How can he sit there, turned on, and do nothing? He said he was a man with no control, yet he has infinitely more authority than I do now.

"What do you want to know?"

He studies me, his eyelids low, hiding himself. "Fort Knox, you are. Why did you come here? What was your plan for this?"

I swallow, my throat dry, and let my body go limp. If I can relax for a moment, maybe some of the need will subside. I focus on him. His sharp cheekbones, bright eyes, and all that ink are telling the world to stay the hell away from him. "I planned to drug you, fuck you, then ask for your help."

"My help with what?"

I swallow and whisper, not trusting he doesn't have ears even here. "To kill my boss."

"The one who told you to drug me in the first place. That's fucked up. Even in my world. Is Priscilla your real name?"

I nod, my head feeling heavier and heavier until I drop it back to the mattress again. The sheets smell like him, but I hadn't noticed until just now. It makes me clench again. "My name is Priscilla Capri."

Ivan slides off the bed like I lit his ass on fire. So he knows my family name then. Makes sense.

"There are no female Capri heirs. I hear they kill females or sell you off in their fucked-up farms as children."

I shove the memories threatening to rise back down into the dark where they belong. "I am not an heir. I'm just the daughter of a lowly illegitimate Capri son. Arthur isn't really acknowledged in the lineage. Nor am I."

Ivan crawls back onto the bed, this time over me. I whimper at the heat and scent of him so close. He slides his knee between my legs until the hard muscle meets my core. "You've done well, *Malyshka*. You can hump my knee this time to get off."

More tears pour down my cheeks, and I squeeze my eyes closed as I press harder against him. Finding a rhythm that gives me what I want takes a minute. Especially since I can't tighten my hold on him with my legs tied down. His warm breath, smelling faintly of vodka, wafts against my face. I let myself retreat, imagining this isn't humiliation but something sexier, deeper, foreplay, maybe. It only takes seconds to detonate again. I'm shaking and gasping when I open my eyes.

He's still hovering over me, his gaze locked on my face. "We aren't done here yet. I wonder what you'll do or tell me if I offer you my cock. Or maybe I'll just fuck that pretty little mouth of yours and forgo your cunt altogether."

I whimper, and he brings his thumb to my lips and presses between them. I suck deep, locking my gaze on his. He might be toying with me, but if he puts his dick in my mouth, it won't be the only thing he wants from me.

"Tell me where the drugs are."

I let him slide his thumb from my mouth and shake my head. "I bought them tonight. I don't know where the stash is."

"No, the ones you had on you, or did you put everything in that glass?"

I blink, terrified to tell him the truth. What will he do with the rest of the drugs? Shit. I can't take much more if he tries to force them down my throat…

I cry in earnest now until he shushes me gently. "It's okay, *Malyshka*, rest. I'll find them myself. It's not like you were wearing much, to begin with."

It takes everything I have to lift my head and watch him gather the dress I'd been wearing. In seconds, he tugs the tiny plastic wrapper from the pocket I'd sewn into the dress myself.

He brandishes it at me. "You didn't even try to hide them. Did you think I'd make an easy mark?"

I shake my head and drop back again, needing to look anywhere but at his devastatingly beautiful face. In my mind, he's the angel of death.

"No," I whisper. "I thought you'd just kill me, and it would all be over. I'd finally be free."

4

IVAN

Of course, the fucking Capri family would come up with something so disgusting. I couldn't even consider all the ways they would use something like this. Outside of apparently attempting to honey trap grown men.

I open the package and try to sniff it without pulling any of the fine white powder into my nose. It's sweet, like baby powder. No fucking thanks.

Cilla is still writhing on the bed, both needing to be touched and trying to free herself from my bonds. It's useless, she's wasting her energy either way, but I stalk back to her side and hold the package out. "What do you know about this drug?"

She moans and rolls her hips, her lower body naked and on full display, but she doesn't care in this state. If I were a nice person, I'd cover her up, but she should have learned before she tangled with me that nothing is nice here. No mercy. No tenderness. Nothing but hard edges to slam your face against.

I grab her chin and hold her face still, forcing her to stare into my eyes. "Tell me what you know about this."

She gasps again and pants. "He calls it SOS. Sex on a stick. He's tested it thoroughly."

I keep my gaze locked with hers and hear what she didn't add at the end of that statement. *On me...*

"Did he lock you up? Give you relief?"

Something shifts behind her eyes. A darkness I can relate to. Finally. Something we have in common. "Not him, no. He threw me to his guards, his scientist, to let me beg them. Let them use me when I couldn't say no."

"Please," she begs. Under any other circumstances, I might have given her what she wanted. Not like this. Not after she tried to drug me. Would she have stood over me while I begged her?

I crouch beside the bed and run my finger up her arm from her wrist. She shifts toward me, pulling the stockings, even as they tighten on her skin so hard they are leaving indentations.

"What else can you tell me about this? Is this the only drug your family makes?"

Her eyes are heavy, and she keeps twisting, trying to get closer. "No. He has many clients, and he designs drugs for them all."

The only way this despicable member of Sal's family could have stayed under the radar was if he had kept well out of the Doubeck territory. But now, with all the power changes in the councils, finding a place we didn't touch was getting harder and harder.

I slip my finger into the pouch, coating it in the drug. When I hold it up to the light, she whimpers, tears pouring down her cheeks in streams. "Please. No. Don't. I can't take anymore."

This time I met her eyes and slid my finger into my mouth along my gum line. It tasted sour, not anything like it smelled. How long would it need to work?

She watches me, eyes wide. "What did you just do? You can't..."

I close the packet and toss it over to the bar. Then I grab another bottle of water, bring it to the bed, and help her drink. "I must say, *Malyshka*, this is one of the more enjoyable interrogations I've conducted. Do you think you've earned my hand this time?"

She thrashes on the bed and stills, a feral smile splitting her lips, making her look almost as mad as I am. "You won't be able to hold back once it hits your system. Just wait. You'll be on me like the beast you are any minute now."

I nod and stand. "Beast, is it? Well, I'm glad to finally know what you truly think of me. Shall we continue?"

Circling to the end of the bed, I press my hands to the comforter and stare up the line of her body. I wish I'd freed her tits before I tied her up, but that could be for later. "What is this like? Explain it to me."

She moans. "It's like…I'm on the edge of an orgasm and can't push myself over. Like my body is begging for it, but it just slips away, out of reach."

"And when I touch you, how does that help?"

I slide my hand over her delicate ankle and up the back of her smooth calf. "It takes some of the edge off. Like maybe that orgasm isn't so unattainable after all."

Gently, I continue up the back of her thigh. "Any touch?"

She nods frantically, biting her lip.

I ease my fingers off her soft, smooth skin and wait for her to wriggle again. Each tug on the bonds is an effort to get to me, to stimulate herself in some way. "One more question for now. Why did you target me?"

She blinks, her hazy eyes going clear for a heartbeat. "No."

I stand and cross my arms over my bare chest. "No?"

While she presses her lips together to keep herself from speaking, she tries to do the same with her thighs, unsuccessfully.

"I won't tell you. You're an asshole."

I chuckle. "That's not news to me, *Malyshka*. I've always been an asshole."

Lightning fast, I move between her spread thighs. She freezes, and I blow a line of cold air on her seeping wet center. She gives me a guttural moan, a noise that reaches inside me and takes hold. "Oh, you could come if I just did that and nothing else. Couldn't you?"

She tilts her hips up, inviting me to touch her.

"Not so fast. Tell me what I want to know…why did you choose me as your target?"

"You're not married," she grates out through clenched teeth.

That's too easy of an answer for how much she resisted. "I think that's only partially true. What else? What weakness could I have shown you to make you think you could get to me?"

I blow another line of cool air on her overheated skin. She claws at the bedding in response and spreads her legs wider. "Tell me, and I'll do it again."

When she stays quiet, I climb off the bed and leave her whimpering through tears. I'll give her a minute to decide to talk while I discuss the development with Kai. I grab my phone from my suit jacket and turn to face her while the call connects.

"Why are you calling me so late?" Kai's voice cuts through the phone.

"Someone tried to drug me tonight."

All sleep is gone now. "Who?" he demands.

"Surprisingly, a pint-size prostitute working in the casino club. I noticed her move and switched the glasses. I'm concerned about these particular drugs being on our streets."

His tone is all business now, and I hear him typing in the background. "Why? What are they doing to her? I assume you have her in your custody, or you wouldn't be calling to talk to me about it."

The long line of her leg keeps drawing my eye. The drugs must be kicking in for me now. My hard-on remains from earlier, so I can't really tell the difference. "The drug is an aphrodisiac. It makes you crazy for sex."

Kai huffs into the receiver softly. "Did you consider maybe she drugged you because she wanted to ride your dick?"

I roll my eyes. "Don't fuck with me, man. I'm not in the mood. Women like her don't want men like me."

His laughter fades slowly, and I wait until he's done ribbing me. "Fine. Did you get any other information?"

"Yes, our friends, the Capri family, at least this particular off-shute, has started something of a designer drug business."

Silence answers me, and I nod. Who's laughing now, motherfucker? "Kai, you there? You understand what I'm saying?"

"Of course, I fucking understand what you're saying. Those council bitches used some kind of drugs on both Michail and me. Could they have come from the Capris?"

Cilla arches on the bed again, trying to touch herself, but she can't reach. No matter how many times she fails, she keeps trying. Admirable, I suppose.

"Maybe. The girl who tried to drug me is the daughter of an illegitimate Capri heir. So Sal's uncle, maybe? How many of these bastards do we have to kill to get them all gone?"

"You still have her?"

I nod, my eyes on her, and then answer. "Yes. She's tied to my bed at the moment."

"You didn't..."

"Fuck you, asshole. I've been interrogating her, but I didn't fuck her, if that's what you're asking. I may be a fucking crazy bastard, but I'm not one of *them*."

With that, I click my phone off and toss it on the couch. My anger rides hot up my throat until all I can think about is smashing things, breaking them open, tearing, shredding, destroying.

I pace back and forth across the width of my room like a lion in a cage. Shit. I need to get out of here before I hurt her, or worse, myself, and leave her like this.

I grab a knife off the table and saw at her bonds in quick swipes. They come loose, and she launches herself at me the second she's free. My knife is up to her throat before I can think about it.

She doesn't seem to care, pressing into the cold steel, a line of red parting her skin as her mouth trails over my jaw and down to my neck.

Something about her mouth on my skin quiets the cold fury Kai built inside me. Turning the solid block of ice in my chest into something molten. But it doesn't matter. I won't fuck her while she's on these drugs. I told Kai I'm not one of them…those people who've used us, degraded us, shamed us. I won't be one of them.

I gently ease her back and strip off her bra in one swipe.

"Please," she begs.

I lift her up, and her legs go around my waist automatically. "Come on, *Malyshka*, let's see if the shower can cool us both down."

I stand us both under the nozzle, turn the handle to cold, and start the spray. She squeaks in my arms and clings to me. After a moment, she blinks down at me, her makeup running down her cheeks. "That's fucking cold. What the fuck?"

I shrug and let the water try to wash away some of the heat roaring inside me. It won't abate while I've got my hands curled around the soft globes of her bare ass or while her tits are so close to licking distance.

This has to be the drugs. I have control over my body, at least sexually.

I drop her to the shower floor, and she glances down. "You're still wearing your boots and your pants."

Fuck. I'd forgotten. I give her some space in my massive shower and rip my boots off. The image of her grinding against them hits me all over again. Then I shuck my pants and kick them away.

Her eyes fly to my achingly hard dick as I grasp it. When she licks her lips, I almost give in. Almost. "Just let me take the edge off. Just a little bit. Please."

I squeeze myself a moment and then release my grasp. She steps forward, but I tug the showerhead out of its socket and hand it to her. "Go to town, sweetheart."

Something like hurt flashes in her eyes, but I don't let it get to me. I pass behind her and out of the shower to grab a towel. I don't need to look back to know she's taken my advice and come hard in seconds.

"It won't help," she says, her voice echoing in the bathroom.

I face her again. "What do you mean?"

"It has to be sex, penetrative sex, or the edge never goes away."

"You can't wait it out?"

She grabs a towel from the stack, her shoulders slumped in defeat. "Eventually, but I can't survive for days like this."

I stalk out of the bathroom and head to my closet. Inside, I snag a box, pull out what I'm hunting for, and throw it on the bed. "Have at it, *Malyshka*. You still haven't earned my cock. No matter how much I want to use it."

5
CILLA

I stare at the light flesh-toned dildo he'd thrown on the bed so haphazardly. And I hated that my pussy clenched on nothing from just the sight of a rigid cock. It's not the fake dick I want. Even though he'd been nothing but an asshole since I walked in the door. Not that I don't deserve it. A hot wash of guilt rolls through my chest, and I clutch the towel tighter above my breasts. I refuse to beg him again. Even with the drugs scorching my body from the inside out, I won't beg him again.

He looks between me and the dildo pointedly. I can hear him saying you are the one who wanted to fuck so badly. Smug fucking bastard. He might be a brute, but I don't think he'd genuinely hurt me. As evident by my still being alive. I expected a gun to the head once he discovered the drugs.

I march to the bed and let my towel fall to the floor. His eyes track from my face slowly—so slowly—down my neck to my breasts, my belly, my neatly trimmed pussy. "See something you like?"

Without answering, he continued his perusal of my naked

body like he had all the time in the world. It would wait for him to look his fill. Maybe the world would wait, but right now, I won't. Not with my face burning red and my body on fire.

I snatch the dildo from the mussed covers and flex my fingers around it. It's a nice quality toy, I'll give him that. I throw him a smirk. "Buy this for yourself, did you? You seem to like them big."

He grabs my hand off the fake dick and wraps it around his real one. "It's a replica. Don't you see the resemblance?"

Tightening my grasp, I explore the hot rigid contours of his flesh. The thick veins running under my delicate skin beg me to sink to my knees and have a taste of him.

The damn drugs are pushing on my senses again, and all I can think about is wrapping my lips around him. He'd fuck my face hard, brutally, until I was choking and crying. He'd have no remorse, and fuck me, I'd love every second.

"What put that look on your face?"

I jerk my hand off his dick and watch it bob against his belly once. Not taking my eyes off it, I answer him. "I was thinking about how good it would feel for you to fuck my face so hard that I'm crying and choking. I want to feel your hot cum in the back of my throat." I let my eyes drift closed, imagining it as everything in my coils up for the thing it's craving.

"Get on the bed," he says, his voice dark.

I snatch up the dildo and glare his way. "Do you mind giving me a little privacy?"

His snort calls me an idiot. "Malyshka, this is my room, and that is my dick you are holding in your hand. My dick you're going to slide into your tight cunt. And I'm going to watch every second of it."

His words push urgency into my blood. Dammit. I need this so badly I can't even think straight. There are a thousand reasons this is such a bad idea, but the thought of being stuck this way, with no true release, for who knows how long, seems unfathomable.

I hate that I've been reduced to this. Every single time. My family, now this asshole. Not one person in the world wouldn't throw me under the bus to get what they want. And most of the time, I end up paying the price. I refuse to look at him while I climb up on the bed.

For my job, I'd make a show of it. Give him what he paid for. But this man gets none of my finesse and none of the skill I've perfected. I roll and lie flat to stare up at the ceiling. At least he's out of my line of sight, and I won't have to see his smug face as I use his dildo to relieve the ache inside me.

Dammit. I hate this so much.

I ease the head of the fake dick through my folds, letting it get nice and slick. I hadn't lied when I'd suggested the dildo is big. It's going to stretch me. It doesn't matter, though, because I love a little bite of pain mixed with my pleasure. The stretch will make it worth the humiliation.

He steps to the side of the bed, staring directly down at me. "What are you waiting for?" His voice is like a whip crack against my skin. Stinging and hot. Dammit.

I tug the end of the dildo down and slip the broad crown around my entrance. It feels so good. Not as good as a living, breathing man between my thighs, but if this is all I'll get, I'll take it.

I squeeze my eyes closed again so I don't have to see him, except I picture his face in my mind. His face hovering over mine to stare into my eyes while he fucks me. He watched my every reaction with each surge into my body, knowing exactly how I like to be fucked.

The rustle of the covers makes me think he's pacing beside the bed. His muscles flex and creek like he's straining them. But I won't look. The image of him in my imagination is better than the real-life man standing beside me. At least far more considerate under the circumstances.

"Faster," he grits out, his tone gravel and guttural. The deep bass adds fuel to my fantasy, making me arch my hips up to meet the wide slide of the dildo into my body. My pussy embraces the sharp pain and the silky pleasure at the same time.

I don't bother stopping the moan that slips out.

A weight settles on the bed next to my thighs, and I freeze. Still keeping my eyes closed. The air stirs above my body, making my nipples pebble against the chill in the room. Is he going to touch me? Should I let him? Will he even give me a choice?

I focus on keeping my back flat on the bed. I still won't beg him. Not for anything. Not for something he already clearly refuses to give me.

When he doesn't do anything, I shake off the sensation of his hip against my thigh and slip the dildo deeper inside me. The silicone balls attached mash against the wetness of my body, but I don't care. I finally have something inside me, and holy hell, it feels so good I give myself over to the fantasy.

In my imagination, Ivan curls his hand around my throat and pins me to the bed while he slides himself into me. It's slow, unhurried like he has all night to fuck me. He never cuts off my air supply, but the heavy weight of his hand in my mind gives me a sense of comfort I've never known.

Then the fantasy and reality merge when the calluses of his palm scratch the sides of my neck. I pop my eyes open, expecting him to be above me, but he's sitting next to me, left hand on my throat, eyes locked on the slow rhythmic pace I've set with the dildo.

"Faster," he orders again.

I clamp my thighs together around my hand to hide the sight of me from him. He doesn't own me. His neck flushes pink, and then he uses his right hand to pry my knees apart and leave them butterflied open on the bed.

I'm panting, both from his rough handling and the dildo still inside me. Now, I'm chasing the orgasm. The faster I come, the faster I can get the hell away from him before I do something stupid like climb him like a tree and beg him to hurt me.

My thighs are slick with my own arousal, and I tense when his fingers curl around the fleshy part of my thigh toward my center. "Slower."

I huff and continue the pace I already set. "A moment ago, you were screaming faster. Now you want slower?"

His hand tightens the tiniest fraction, and it's enough to steal any other words in my head. The clench of his fingers is enough to start the long fall toward my orgasm. When he tosses my hand off the dildo and seizes it, I almost come right then. One of his hands locked on my throat, the other slowly, achingly slow, sliding the silicone dick inside me. But he doesn't leave it. He pulls it almost completely out so I can feel the wide crown pressing back into my entrance with a slight sting. "Fuck," I groan, unable to maintain my composure. No. My pride when this shit is happening right now.

"I thought you said you weren't going to fuck me," I choke out, his palm constricting my voice slightly.

He doesn't answer, as if his entire being is focused on fucking me with the fake dildo. I snap my hands up to grab at it. To stop this. But he slaps them away. Again, I try to take it. This time he leans down to align his face with mine, his hand squeezing tighter. "I said fucking no. Now lie still while I fucking ruin that beautiful cunt."

It's on the tip of my tongue to invite him to do it with his own dick, but I can't get a word out due to the strength of his grip. I can still breathe, but speaking is useless.

He pumps the cock into me faster, my channel gripping

along the ridges. I'm so close to coming, and a hot tear leaks out of the corner of my eye. I need it more than I need to breathe right now.

Like he can read my mind, he increases the pace and changes the angle, so the top of the dildo grazes near my clit. It's not much but combined with everything else. With the slightly spicy scent of his skin, the rough calluses on his palm, the way he's so transfixed by my body. All of it sends me down the spiral of the most violent orgasm I've ever had. It wrecks me, burning and rebuilding as it rolls through my body. Every inch of me quakes in his grasp.

"Yes," he whispers. "Take my cock like a good little girl, and I might give you a reward."

His eyes are shiny, and I can tell he's in the heaviest and hardest part of the drug now. In a moment, he'll get sluggish, literally aching with the need to fuck anything that is moving.

"Ivan," I whisper, trying to draw his attention, but he's still focused on the dildo as he eases it gently in and out of me. I try to pry his hand loose enough to speak properly, but his grip is like iron. He could choke me out in a few seconds, and I'd be powerless to stop him.

For some reason, that makes me roll my hips up into the dildo, needing more of this. I need more of him.

The door bursts open in a crash, but he doesn't even glance up. I look over and catch sight of the men who should have arrived sooner. Shit. They're here because of me.

What have I done, condemning him to a fate I've lived with for years? For my freedom...

Dammit. I can't do this. I open my mouth to warn Ivan, but one of the guards is already at his neck, a needle inserted, and the plunger depressed.

Ivan wavers on his feet, and I swear I caught hurt in his eyes before he closes them and sinks to the floor in a way too beautiful heap.

A guard throws my dress at me. "Get dressed. The boss will want to see you."

I glare at him, sliding the shirt over my head. "Tell *the boss* he can go fuck himself. I've earned my freedom."

A sharp sting in my neck, and the room goes dark before I get another word out.

6

IVAN

The darkness is absolute. I blink my eyes open, trying to latch onto any shape or light in the room, but there's no use. Not even a sliver of light around a window or a door. I haven't been inside a fully dark room since I was a child. Nightmares of monsters in the closet and under the bed were beaten out of me until the darkness became another kind of hiding place.

Memories filter back to me. Priscilla laid out so beautifully on my bed, her soft thighs spread wide just for me. No. That's not true. She'd done it for whoever is pulling her strings. Her father, perhaps, which brings far more disturbing questions to mind.

A pounding starts in my head, so I lean against the cold wall, letting the chill sink in. It feels like brick, and they've got me secured with my arms up with maybe zip ties. I can't see the material, but it doesn't make much noise when I move and has barely any give.

It doesn't matter, though. I'll get out of here soon enough. Either on my own or when Kai and the others come for me. No one can stay out of touch and under the radar long enough that Kai couldn't track them eventually.

A light flickers over the door, starting dim and growing brighter for a minute. Someone must be coming for a little chat. Perfect.

I scan the room, but there's nothing in the small space. It looks like someone's storage unit, but it's empty save for one metal chair and a table a few feet in front of the door. Looks like someone doesn't want to get too close to his visitors.

I keep looking around and spot a camera near the ceiling at the corner where the walls meet. It's pointed directly at me, and a small red light is on the front. Oh yeah, someone is watching me. "Priscilla," I call. "Are you in there, *Malyshka*? I'm going to kill you for this. I hope you know that. I don't care how pretty your pussy is."

There doesn't seem to be any kind of speakers that I can see, so I don't expect an answer.

"Or should I be calling out to Arthur Capri? I believe you're running this show. Arrrrrrttttthhhhurrrrr...come play with me, Arthur. I promise you'll see your own organs before you die slowly."

One of the many problems with the Capri family is that they are so damn proud. Not a single one of them could let a taunt like that slide. Not without repercussions, and usually with the opponent incapacitated before they take their cheap shot.

My arms are numb. How long could I have been restrained here before I woke? I'm not hungry. Maybe a little thirsty, but that could be due to the drug combinations running through my system.

"Arthur," I bark out. "Stop being a fucking asshole who sends a woman, a member of his family, to do his own dirty work and speak to me like a man."

There we go. Nothing a Capri family member hates more

than emasculation. I personally think it's why they target so many children. They are vulnerable and can't fight back.

I keep my eyes on the camera even if the angle makes my neck ache. "Priscilla, you in there, baby? You could come talk to me too. I'm sure your daddy could spare you a while to entertain his new guest."

Taunt after taunt, and no one comes. Eventually, I lapse into silence as my throat grows drier and drier. I can always start again once someone comes in to engage. They obviously want something from me, or else I'd be dead already. Why take a prisoner when you can kill him instead?

I shift my legs on the concrete floor as my ass goes numb along with my arms. At least someone put some underwear on me before they dragged me into this shit hole. My own underwear, at that. Something tells me Priscilla had a hand in it. The men who removed me from my room likely wouldn't have given a shit if I was bare-ass naked.

The light on the camera blinks a few times, and I keep my gaze pinned on it. Did Kai hack their systems already, or was someone finally going to come in and talk to me?

I glare at the lens, making sure the person on the other side can see I'll rip them apart piece by piece when I get out of this box.

The door across from me creaks open slowly. It looks like heavy steel, even though I'm not at a great angle for the best view. A tall, willowy man, maybe in his fifties, enters the room and sits across from me. At least three feet are between my farthest stretch and his shiny black shoes, so there's no use trying to attack him.

I eye his out-of-date, ill-fitting suit. "Arthur, I presume?"

He dips his head and gives my mostly naked body the same perusal. "Since we are going by first names already, I'll call you Ivan."

I swallow the bile climbing up the back of my throat and keep staring into his cold, dull eyes. "You can call me your murderer if that sounds better to you."

"Cute. But we aren't here to discuss my evisceration. I have a very specific task in mind for you."

He's doing the villain monologue thing, so I sit back and wait for him to describe his dastardly plans.

"You see, Ivan, you've been somewhat of a nuisance to me lately. On the one hand, you and your little friends are doing a wonderful job weeding the world of some of my less savory family members. On the other hand, you are interfering with my business. That is something I do not tolerate."

The silence stretches, and I sigh. "Oh, you're done. Cool. Is this the part where you threaten to kill me, or the part where you actually try to kill me? At least your other family member got close enough to make her attempt. Much much closer than you are right now. Are you afraid of me, Arthur?"

His eyes are cold and flat as he continues to look at me. "Does a horse need to fear an ant? No, Ivan, I have no fear of you or your kind. I'll be rid of you all soon enough anyway."

"Great, then do it already. What are you waiting for?"

His eyes narrow, and he leans forward to brace his elbows on his wrinkled slacks. "You don't fear death? What about pain? Do you fear that?"

I give him my most unhinged smile. I let him see how far the darkness has permeated me. "Do I look like I fear death? Pain is only another word for living, and I've dealt with more of it than you will ever know."

Arthur waves his hand and sits back in his chair again. "Oh, well then, I suppose this experiment will be extra interesting. I look forward to breaking you, Ivan. The strongest ones are usually the quickest to fall."

I let his words roll around in my head. He plans to torture

me, or he's given me more of his perverse drugs. Hell, he could do both at the same time if he managed to get the dosage right.

Now that we've sat back to silently contemplate each other, I can see Priscilla in his features. Maybe she's his niece or his sister. Much much younger sister.

Arthur cuts through my thoughts with a huff. "Oh, please forgive me. I forgot to introduce you."

The door behind him opens slowly, and someone stumbles into the room on bare feet. She turns, and I catch sight of her creamy thighs and delicate hands. Her face is still flushed, and her eyes go wide as she finally turns to look at me. I stare her down as she keeps as much distance as possible from the man in the chair and me. He reaches out and jerks her toward him by her bicep. "Priscilla, dear, don't be rude to our guest."

She clears her throat, clearly recoiling from his hold. "We've already met, as you well know."

Arthur cuts a fake laugh. "Oh, of course, how silly of me. You two haven't just met. By the reports my men gave me, they found you both quite cozy."

I shift my gaze to him and let him see the contempt I feel. "Well, your drugs were effective, I suppose. But if you are asking if I fucked her? No. I didn't. She's nothing but your little plaything, and I don't want anything to do with Capri's sloppy seconds."

For the first time since I don't know when, I feel a sharp spike of guilt in my chest. It's not true. I still want to drag her onto my lap and fuck all the rage out of me. I want to rip my arms from the socket to cross the room and keep her safe. Even if she doesn't deserve it.

Arthur chuckles softly and drags the girl closer. Her soft pink sweater and black sweatpants aren't enough to disguise how much she hates his touch. "Oh, well, if she doesn't, please you, I have many more girls you might try out. I guess you won't be calling me Papa anytime soon, then."

I narrow my eyes. Keeping the rest of my face blank as I consider his words. Papa?

But the asshole doesn't miss anything. Not one damn thing. Interesting. A member of the Capri family who might actually be worth going head-to-head with. All the rest of them are whimpering fools. Would this one cry when I showed him his own intestines? For once, I was more curious than anything else. I gave in to the feeling. "Papa? Is that your twist on Daddy because I assure you there's not a man alive who could get me to call him Daddy and live to survive afterward."

Arthur only curls his lips up in another enigmatic smile. "Oh, he hasn't figured it out yet, Cilla, dear. Do you want to tell him, or should I? This is going to be so much more fun now."

Priscilla keeps trying to get out of his hold, and in response, Arthur only tightens his grip further. I'm about five seconds from ripping my own hand off just to get to her and remove his. She didn't do me any favors but back in my room, for a few seconds, she chased away the darkness enough that I could think.

My demons are back in full force now, though, and the darkest part of me can't wait to unleash them on the entire Capri family. I'll kill them all. Anyone even remotely associated with the Capri's won't survive their mistake.

Arthur's voice cuts through the red rage rolling through my head. "He does brood beautifully, doesn't he, darling? Since you aren't going to tell him, I suppose I should do the honors."

Priscilla gives one last attempt to get out of his grip and then stands her ground, her chin hiked up. She doesn't meet my eye when she speaks, and her voice is barely a whisper. "This is my boss. The man who sent me to drug you."

The man she wants me to kill. Interesting.

But by the gleeful expression on Arthur's face, I know there is more he can't wait to reveal. "Go on, dear. Finish the introductions."

She stays silent, and Arthur squeezes her arm until she lets out a soft, pained moan. Then he shoves her so hard she bodily bounces off the wall beside him. He barely spares her a glance as she regains her footing.

His cold, dead eyes are on me now. "You didn't think I'd send just anyone to grab one of Adrian Doubeck's revered Five, did you? This is my daughter, Priscilla."

I flashback to the hotel room when she mentioned her boss and being the daughter of an illegitimate Capri heir. She even told me his name, which I remembered, but why couldn't I remember the rest of it?

Arthur laughs softly. "He understands now, my darling. Let's get the first drug round ready for our new friend."

She spares me one last glance and precedes her father to the door.

Fuck. Too bad. She'll have to die with the rest of them after all.

7
CILLA

I should have known I'd never be free of this place. Free of my father. Agreeing to do something so terrible to Ivan gave them leverage over me. All they have to do is lock us up together so he can take his revenge, and I'll be a problem no one has to deal with anymore.

I stare at the wall across from my sad mattress on the floor. It's barren, so why bother decorating when they move around so much. I mostly live out of the duffel bag at the end of the bed these days. The outfits I own are all easy to shake the wrinkles out of. My work clothes are kept in the closet so, at the very least, I can look presentable when I go there.

If I had a choice, I wouldn't be a prostitute, but it did give me the chance to stash away some money to eventually escape. My father might still chase me down, but I might be able to get a few days of freedom before he drags me back and punishes me.

A heavy thud hits my door, and the wood slams open into the wall behind it. Nothing surprises me anymore, so I stay on my palette and stare up at the angry eyes of my father.

He kicks at the mattress. "What the hell are you doing still in bed? We have work to do."

I swallow hard to buy myself a minute so I don't snap out an answer and get hurt. "What kind of work? I thought I did my part."

His scowl is answer enough. It not only called me an idiot but promised pain if I didn't get up right now. Yet I stay huddled under my thin blanket, unable to move. I know he wants to drag me back to that cell, and I can't face Ivan again. Not after what I've done to him.

"Get the hell up, girl. I don't have time for this. What's your problem? Are you sick?"

The drugs are still swirling through me, but that's not what he means. It wouldn't matter if my brains were leaking out of my ears. He'd still expect me to perform whatever menial task he has in mind. "I'm fine."

He crouches down, putting him closer to me. His Old Spice scent is enough to make me gag, but I keep it together.

"Did you fuck him? Is that what this is about?"

I shake my head against the pillow. "No, we didn't get that far."

"Oh, I'm well aware. My guys told me exactly how far you got and still have to go."

That snaps me fully awake. "Wh-What?"

"You didn't fuck him. I want you to do that, and I want you to make it so good he can't stand being without his dick inside you."

I mean, I'm not terrible-looking, but somehow, I think he can resist my charms in my current state. Before I can think of an answer, he stands and paces back and forth beside my bed, one wall to one wall in my tiny bedroom that is more like a glorified closet.

"I want you to fuck him, and I want you to get the information I need from him."

It's on the tip of my tongue to tell him no. To try to figure a way out of this, but no matter what I say, it won't matter. Once he gets stuck on a course of action, he sticks with it until his plan is complete. And whatever he has planned for Ivan can't be good.

I sit up in bed and hug my blankets to my chest even though I'm in my ratty pajamas. "Don't you have another girl? Someone he will like better?"

He waves his hand, still lost in thought. "Oh, we tried several girls and a couple of guys, but he didn't bite on any of them. None of them inspired the rage you brought out in him. It has to be you and no one else. I think if I send you back in there, you'll be able to get anything I want out of him."

"And what's that? What can he possibly know that sex will get him to confess to me?"

He turns his cold eyes on me, and I resist the urge to shrink away. "Did I ask you for your opinion on this? I don't believe I did."

Like a cobra, he strikes out, the back of his hand connecting with my cheek. It's so fast I don't have time to react. My face goes sideways, and I know that strike was hard enough to leave a visible bruise. It hurts, but I'm beyond crying at his abuse. It only makes him want to hit me more. "Can you at least tell me what you want me to get out of him? So I can try to lead him to the right answers?"

He's gone back to his pacing, not answering, and I'm repeating over and over in my mind my wish for him to leave the room and let me be in peace for a while.

When he stops pacing, he turns to face me, his hands tucked tightly behind his back in the classic military at ease position. "I want to know about the drugs his family runs. I want to know how close they are to bringing down the main branch of our family, and I want to know what it will take to get him on my side."

I blink. He's got to be crazy. Adrian Doubeck's men are unturnable. It's a well-known fact that his people are as loyal to him as family. Not that family or blood mean much in our world.

I gently press my fingers to my cheek to check the tenderness. "Any way I get a choice in this?"

He raises his hand like he's going to hit me again, his eyes narrowing. I flinch back this time to protect my face, but he stops and then drops his hands, contempt in his gaze. "Remember where you come from, girl, and remember where I can send you if you don't obey me."

At this point, maybe the graveyard wouldn't be so bad. I don't know how much more I can take of playing whore for my father to trade and sell away. It disgusts me. I want out so bad, and it's the only reason I attempted to tangle with Ivan.

I keep the distance between us and stare away from him now. "Anything else?"

He makes a non-committal noise and heads to the door. On the way out, he calls, "Try not to die on your first interrogation, pumpkin."

The nickname makes bile rise in my throat. I lie on the pillow and roll away from the door to face the other empty white wall. Maybe things will go better for me on this track. I couldn't win my freedom on my own, but Ivan could offer a different kind of freedom. If he kills me, I won't have to be here anymore and face the consequences of my choices. If I was going to die, I'd rather it be at his hand than my father's or one of his guards. Who knew what they would do to my body after my soul fled.

I remember the strong feel of his hands on my skin. Yeah, it won't take much for him to snap and get his revenge.

I shuffle off the bed and drag my duffel closer to my legs so I can grab some clean clothes. Once I pull the shirt over my head, I gather my hair up in a messy bun. Then I slip into a worn pair of jeans and head into my small ensuite to brush my teeth and wash my face.

My father probably wants me in my prostitute costume so I can entice his prisoner, but if I'm dying today, I'm doing it looking like myself. None of the makeup and fake clothes. Clothes I'd rather burn than wear again.

After I'm done in the bathroom, I hunt down my phone and text the supervisor at the casino to let them know I won't be back at work tonight. I get a winky face emoji in return. Well, she must know who I walked out with last night. And if that's the case, maybe one of his friends will be able to find him before my father can really get his mad scientist on.

I toss the phone onto my bed and slide my feet into a pair of canvas slip-ons. This is as good as it's going to get today, and if anyone has a problem with it, they will have to drag me back to my room themselves. It's funny how much less scared I am of all of my father's men when I've faced Ivan's anger and survived. Once, at least.

My room is on the basement level so my father can keep his eyes on me. Which makes it easy to walk down the long compound hallway to get to the dungeon cells. A guard stands outside, Pavil something, I think. I don't know his face as he's not one of the men who have taken advantage of my father's generous offerings of my body to his guards.

I grit my teeth as I approach him, and he casts his eyes down and then back up at the wall.

With a sigh, I wave at the door. "I'm supposed to have a conversation with our prisoner in there."

He straightens his spine, his black shirt tightening across his chest at the movement. Right now, he thinks he's being respectful of me. Pretty soon, he'll follow in the other guards' footsteps and treat me like garbage along with everyone else.

"Are we going to stand here in the hallway all day, or are you going to unlock the door for me?"

One of the other guards. Eric. Tall, beautiful, disturbingly evil Eric strides down the hall with a tray of food in his hands. He stops beside Pavil and thrusts the tray at my chest hard enough to send me back a few steps. "We already got him cleaned up and changed for you, princess. Go give him some attention, and we'll keep an eye on things from the video screens."

I swallow against another wave of bile, my throat burning, and clutch the tray, so he will take a step back and release it. When I don't respond to him, he grabs my chin hard and tilts my face up.

His sneer is enough to make me look away so I don't have to see it. "You didn't even bother to put on some makeup? He's not going to want you looking like this. You're like a fucking kindergarten teacher or some shit."

I know better than to respond. It will only make him more violent and more brutal. After a few tense seconds, he releases my face with a little shove and steps back to look at Pavil. "What the fuck are you looking at?"

Pavil narrows his eyes but doesn't comment on Eric's behavior or his question.

Once Eric turns and heads back down the hallway toward the control room, I face Pavil. "Can you open the door now?"

He reaches into his pocket, fumbling with something, then slips a glass vial I recognize all too well into the coin pocket of my jeans. "Just in case you need some help in there. The doc was just in there, though, so he might already have what he needs."

I stare him down this time. My patience has blown its limits and kept on going. Now all I have left is numbness. It's comforting, actually. Better than the abject despair I usually feel as I cry myself to sleep at night.

Pavil opens the heavy steel door, and I step into the semi-dark room to face my death for the last time.

8

IVAN

The steel door doesn't scrape against the concrete this time. It does squeak ever so slightly on the hinges as it opens and then closes. I don't need to look up to know who entered. She's silent as if she's spent her entire life walking carefully, trying not to draw attention to herself.

I keep my eyes downcast so she can't tell if I'm asleep or not. Her feet move closer, on the edge of my vision. The spiteful part of me is tempted to kick out, bring her to her knees, and make her pay for what she's done to me. But I don't. Something about her calms me. Until I figure it out, I refuse to hurt her, well, at least no more than she wants to be hurt by me.

I slowly raise my eyes enough that I can keep her in my sight. She might have some kind of sway over me, but I sure as shit don't trust her. Or her crazy ass father. How could she have stayed with him this long, knowing what he's done, participated in it, or hell, been one of his victims? She could have come to us in the casino and spilled everything at any time. We'd have protected her. But I guess, given the stories that circulate about the five, maybe she feared our response more than her father's.

She's in jeans today, and a T-shirt with a hole at her waist, giving me glimpses of pale skin in the shadows. Her breasts aren't on display like the other night, but I like this look on her more. The tight T-shirt outlines every curve, forcing me to keep going until I meet her eyes. Her blond hair is stacked on her head with a rubber band, and she's not wearing any makeup. In fact, she looks like she rolled out of bed and came straight here.

A few heartbeats pass as we lock eyes, and she gently sets the tray between my splayed knees and retreats until her back hits the table.

Well, if they plan to use me as a guinea pig, I suppose they need to keep me alive. Although, I'd prefer a different plan. One where they just put me down because the second I'm free, all of these motherfuckers are going down hard.

Including her. Especially her. I might even take my time and make it hurt with her. It's her fault I'm here after all.

I keep staring her down, letting her see through the mask into the heart of rage that always boils inside me. I let her see exactly how much I hate her fucking Capri guts.

"You the help now? From the little show you and your daddy put on before, it seemed more like you're in on this together."

A soft huff slips out of her, and she slides around the edge of the small steel table to put it between us. I lift my shoulders and wiggle my tingling fingers at her. "One of you geniuses better figure out what you want because I can't fucking feed myself zip-tied to a wall."

She scans my body. The bruises on my ribs and down to the erection, tenting my black boxer briefs.

"Don't worry, *Malyshka*, that's not for you. I'd rather fuck a rusty tin can than you right now. Unless you want to bring that pretty little ass over here and cut me free. You do that, and I might forgive what's happened between us."

She clears her throat and then shakes her head, sending her

blond bun wiggling. "No, I'm sorry. I can't unlock you. I don't have a way to cut those ties, and even if I did, he'd kill me for letting you go. He made it seem like I'm helping him more than I am. I promise I wouldn't have done this if there was any other way."

Oh good, she's a talker when she's nervous and a talker when she wants to fuck. Her sweet begging as she spread her thighs comes to mind, and I have to grit my teeth against the pulse in my dick. "Any other way to do what?"

She takes a tentative step forward, her hand trailing the top of the table until she reaches the edge closer to me. "To be free. To get out of this hellhole and have a normal life."

Did she mention that before? I can't remember between the drugs and the haze her body awoke in me. "So you drugged me to earn your own freedom?"

Her pretty eyes narrow, and she sucks her full bottom lip between her teeth. "Actually, if you recall, I didn't drug you. You drugged me. I remember this very vividly, considering how you deigned to torture me to get information."

I roll my eyes and drop my head against the unforgiving rock behind me. "I recall giving you exactly what you needed every time you begged me. And oh, how you fucking begged. Beautifully, might I add."

She squares her shoulders, her chin lifting. "Well, I hope you remember it well because that's the last time you'll hear it from me."

I snort, lazily sliding my gaze down her body. "You think so, but I promise you'll beg me again soon. Now come over here and feed me, or are you just going to leave the tray out of reach and hope I can feed myself with my magical mind powers."

For a heartbeat, she looks like she might be considering I could bewitch her, but then she shakes her head and steps forward between my spread feet. "I could leave you like this since you're being an asshole. Because you did the same to me last night. They would feed you eventually. Someone would."

I let her see how much I fucking care whether I eat or not. It doesn't matter since the food is likely drugged anyway.

She sighs loudly and takes another step forward to move the tray to the other side of my leg. Then she neatly folds her body to sit on her heels between my thighs. My dick suddenly feels tighter, like I might explode if I don't get inside her. But I'm not an animal despite what these people think of me. And it's clear she doesn't want to touch any part of me.

She grabs the spoon in the soup and then holds her hand under it as she guides it to my face. I can't resist. I snap out with my teeth, making her jerk back, spilling the soup down my chest and stomach.

It's not even warm, so I'm not worried about it. There's a wounded look in her eyes, then she glares. "I'm trying to be nice, asshole. I should just let you rot in here until they drug you to death and leave you in a puddle of your own cum."

The corner of my mouth lifts before I can reconsider. "Oh, baby has a bit of bite to her. Where were all those teeth last night?"

She swallows and looks down at the tray, pulls off the edge of a roll, and shoves it hard between my lips. I'm full-on smiling now as I watch her. Oh yes. I like her like this. Fight and fury. My dick is somehow getting even harder. I want to fuck that fight out of her. I want her at my feet, begging for more. Begging for mercy.

I chew the food and grin at her while I imagine how to make her scream in all the ways I want.

Her face goes pink in the dim lighting. "Stop looking at me like that."

I swallow. "Like what?"

She shrugs and grabs another chunk of bread. This time she

offers it, and I tug it from her grasp to chew. "I don't know. Like you want to eat me, or you want to *eat* me."

"Where's the fun in knowing which before we actually play."

Her hand shakes as she offers more food. I chew slowly, watching the blush in her cheeks wash down her neck. I bet her chest and tits bear that same pretty pink hue.

When I don't bite her, she grabs the spoon and feeds me a bit of the soup. It's cold but tastes fine. I've had worse.

She darts her eyes around while she feeds me as if she doesn't want to spend too long looking at me directly. Is it guilt or something else? It pisses me off that I can't tell.

"What is it, *Malyshka*? I can see something going in that brain of yours. You reveal everything with your eyes."

She blinks and drops her gaze to my mouth while I take the next bite of food. "I was just wondering if you are what they say you are."

I know what she means. The animal. "You're the one who tried to drug me and came to my room, and you don't know? You didn't think it was a risk?"

She shakes her head, her shoulders sagging away from her ears. "No, whether I succeeded or you killed me, I'd be free either way."

As if she's had enough of me, this room, and her life all at once, she rises gracefully and grabs the tray off the floor. But she only sits it on the table and turns to look down at me. "You need your strength. Do whatever you can to keep it. They will try to break you over and over. It's something my father enjoys doing most of all. The stronger the will, the more satisfying it is for him."

I narrow my eyes at her. Does she know from personal experience? "Did he break you?"

She drops her gaze to the tray and arranges the contents as if she needs something to do with her hands. "A long time ago. I'll never be free of him, and he will make sure I know that even more now."

I can already feel the anger creeping back inside me. As if it had drawn away from her light, but the farther she gets from me, the closer it stalks. "Wait, stay for a second."

She freezes, hand poised over the handles of the tray. "What do you want?"

"How is this going to go? What will he do next?"

When she meets my eyes, tears rim the corners of hers. "He's going to drug you. I'm sure it was in the food. He's going to use you to test his little mad science experiments. Worse, he'll let the guards use you until no part of you feels like your own anymore. Then he'll hurt you and repeat the cycle until you no longer care whether you live or die."

I hiss out a breath. "Well, shit. I guess I've got something to look forward to."

She doesn't laugh. Or smile. Or cry. Her shimmering eyes track from my face down my body to my feet and back again. "I hope you survive. It's my fault you're here, and since it didn't work anyway, I regret you're suffering for it."

I grin, trying to keep the rage at bay. The striking, coiling, angry thing inside me wants to snap out and hurt her. "Was that an apology, *Malyshka*? You could say you're sorry with your mouth on my dick, and maybe I'd be more inclined to believe it."

Her shoulders settle back, and she cuts me one last glare and grabs the tray. It's on the tip of my tongue to call her back. The anger rises in me with every step she takes toward the door.

I won't beg, though. I don't beg. And she's definitely not the one who can make me do it.

The lights go out, and the darkness settles around me once more. A fitting atmosphere for the anger tinting my vision red. The second I'm out of my bonds, they'll all be dead.

9

CILLA

There are so many places in the house I can hide. My room is the first place anyone would look for me, but I don't feel remotely safe anywhere else. There's not much space, my mattress, closet, and a tiny bathroom, so I stay huddled on my bed with the blanket pulled over my face. It won't be long until my father sends one of his men to come and grab me. Put me to work. I know exactly what he has planned for Ivan, and I don't want to be a part of it anymore.

The guilt that he is locked up down there, and I'm here, relatively safe in my bed, is eating me alive. I did that to him. Not alone, sure, but I doubt it would have happened without my help.

I try not to think about what they are doing to him down there. My father is probably in his lab, deep in mad scientist mode concocting the worst drug combo imaginable to target Ivan's physiology specifically. Designer drugs at their most evil. He does that often. Comes up with the perfect poison for whatever job is needed. Not just for lust or ecstasy but for assassinations and murders too. He's created drugs that mimic the drugs the target is already taking, so it looks like a self-inflicted overdose. So I can't even imagine what he wants with Ivan.

There's only so long I can stay bunkered down in my room. Eventually, they will make me talk to him. Talk to him, seduce him, drug him, whatever is needed to get the information my father wants. For now, though, maybe there is some way I can help him. At least until the next part comes. He'll be stronger for it, more able to resist.

I shove off the covers and sit with my knees up, waiting. The guards should be changing soon, and it will be my best chance to sneak into the room with him. The camera doesn't stay on the entire time, and even if the guards leave it on, no one ever watches it unless my father is conducting an experiment in the cell.

I watch the clock on my phone move slowly. Ten minutes feels like ten hours before I wobble to my feet and exit into the hall. With the guard change, the halls are empty. They usually meet in the garage to do a pass-down briefing, so I have a few minutes until anyone spots me.

My hands are shaking as I quietly unlatch the door and slip inside. It's pitch dark the second the little sliver of light is cut off by the heavy steel.

"What are you doing here?" His voice is deeper, grating as if he's been screaming.

My heart shoots into my throat, and I have to clear it before I can speak. "I'm here to help you. At least as much as I can while you're stuck here." I refrain from adding that it's my fault. He knows who to blame, and I don't want him any more riled than I'm sure he already is.

It takes several minutes to tiptoe across the floor, skirting the table and chairs, to get to the other side. Earlier, his feet were only a few feet from the table. But with the chill in the air, I hope he's huddled up some, at least.

I crouch, and my hand meets the warm bare skin of his ankle. "Are you cold?"

"What the fuck do you care if I'm cold? You didn't bring any clothes with you, did you?"

I shake my head and then remember he can't see me. Nor the hot blush in my cheeks at my stupidity. "No. I didn't bring you any clothes. I only had a few minutes to get in here while the guards changed."

He shifts his feet to tug out of my grasp. "Scissors, a knife, a hacksaw, a .45, anything that might help me get out of this fucking cage?" His voice is too soft, too controlled.

My mind screams to step back and get the hell away from him, but the guilt in my belly won't allow me to move. "No. I didn't bring anything with me. It's just me. I can't let you go. They'll kill me."

"Isn't that what you wanted anyway? For me to kill you?"

I shuffle forward in my crouch, but I don't feel him. "If you kill me, I know, at least, I think I know, it would have been quick. If my father kills me, he'll give me to his men, and they will use me until someone finally kills me by accident."

He doesn't speak, but I can hear him breathing, or maybe that's my ragged breath. Between the nerves and the fear of being caught, I can't catch a full breath. I slide my hand along the cold hard floor, but I still feel nothing. Carefully, I keep creeping closer in the dark, hoping I'll reach him. At the very least, I can give him some of my body heat.

"Are you okay? Have they hurt you yet?"

There's a long pause, and then he finally answers, and I shift my face, trying to see him in the dark. "No. But they forced a shit ton of drugs down my throat earlier. It took three of them, and I'm sure one had to go to the hospital. I hope he's dead." The calm neutral way he says it makes my palms sweat despite the chill.

"Good. I hate those guys. They should all be dead."

I keep moving until my hand finally meets warm skin again, and then in a lightning flash, I realize I crawled between his sprawled open legs, and my hand is now pressed against his stomach. His erection pokes my wrist.

I jerk away. "Sorry. Sorry, I can't see anything."

"What do you want, Priscilla?" He draws my name out like he's taunting me. Like he knows I don't like it.

"If they gave you the same drugs I tried to, why aren't you trying to fuck the concrete right now?" I reach out and run my hand against his abs again.

He hisses out a long breath. Ah. Not as unaffected as he's pretending to be.

"Just because I have more self-control doesn't mean I want your fucking hands on me."

His knee hits the side of my hip hard enough to send me sprawling to my ass. I have to catch myself before my face hits the floor. "What the fuck? I came here to help you."

"Oh, how do you plan to do that? You didn't bring me anything I can use, and you sure as hell didn't bring me any weapons. How were you planning to help me?" He's angry now, and it should scare the shit out of me. I've seen him angry with the casino before. The ambulance barely made it in time to help the other guy.

"I can warm you up some, maybe. I thought if they had been drugging you, and you needed relief." I wobble over onto my feet again, keeping a little more distance between us this time. "I'm just trying to help the only way I'm able. If I free you, they will torture and kill me in the worst way possible. I can't do it. I'm sorry."

I reach out to touch him again, but he jerks his thigh from

under my fingers. "Don't fucking touch me. I told you." He's on the verge of screaming now, and if he doesn't keep quiet, one of the guards will come in and catch me here.

I scramble over his thick muscled thighs and straddle him. With a whispered apology, I put my hand over his mouth. I'm close enough now that I can see his eyes and every bit of hate he harbors for me in those dark depths. "I'm so sorry, but I can't let you bring the guards. I'll leave you in a minute once they go for their first coffee break. I just have to wait until then."

I try not to think of his thick length pressed between us. My threadbare black leggings are doing nothing to dampen the feel of him against me. His hips press up to rub himself there, and I clamp my mouth together so I don't moan.

Gently, I loosen my hand over his mouth. "If I drop this, are you going to calm down? You can say whatever you need to say, but I just can't get caught here."

His eyes promise pain, but I hold my ground. Finally, he shakes his head.

Well then.

I blink and shift forward so I can see him better in the dark. He gives me nothing, though. No way to tell what he's thinking or feeling besides massively aroused between my thighs.

I swallow the lump in my throat and try to stay still. "Do you want me to take care of it for you?"

He shakes his head and winces as my knee catches the waistband of his underwear. No doubt the fabric feels like sandpaper right now. I use my free hand to rip down the edge of his boxer briefs, freeing his cock between us. He hisses a slow breath, and it feels hot against my palm.

"Better?"

One curt nod is all he gives me.

God, how did we end up in this position? Him a drugged prisoner, and me straddling his lap so wet I can barely keep still.

He leans forward until our foreheads are almost touching, and the back of my hand is pressed against my lips. "I can smell you," he whispers against my skin.

Fucking hell. No. It's not right to be turned on now. Not while this isn't his choice. He shifts this time, sliding himself along my center. I lean forward, almost falling into his chest completely under the sensual assault.

He does it again but then stops. I freeze over him, absolutely not thinking about riding his cock into oblivion to give us both relief.

"Fist me with your hand, but you don't get off. You still don't deserve my cock." The words are garbled behind my hold, but I still catch them all.

I grab him tight in my free hand and pump him a few times, getting a feel for how he likes to be touched. Hard, rough, just as I suspected. I grip him tighter and clench my thighs around his so I don't rub against him more than necessary.

I go to move my hand and use both of them, but he shakes his head. So I clamp my hand against his mouth tighter, and he curses in muffled abandon as I keep jerking him off. I'm so wet that I'm sure he could see it on my leggings if the room wasn't so dark. I want to lift up and slide him inside me, take him deep enough that it hurts, and let him have his way with my body.

Of course, I don't. I'll respect his wishes, but fucking hell, I need him inside me like I need to breathe.

He lifts his hips to meet my hand now. "Faster."

I oblige, shifting to get a better grip even though it's not my dominant hand. It only takes another minute until he's groaning, his hot cum pouring over my knuckles and legs. Shit. I didn't think this part through.

I let him go and carefully move my fingers to take off my shirt, then the sports bra underneath. Quickly, I use the bra to clean us both up and tug my shirt back over my head.

Once I'm done, I glance up, but he's on me, his teeth in the side of my neck so hard if I move, he'd rip skin. I shudder under the primal bite until he releases me and leans back, his eyes closed. "Get the fuck out."

10

IVAN

No telling how long they've kept me locked up in this hellhole. I can feel the anger burning and eating its way through my sanity. Soon all they will find is the animal they believe me to be. It doesn't matter, though. There isn't a single person I don't want to rip to shreds with my bare hands. Not a single person here doesn't deserve the violence riding my mind and body.

I try to shift on the cold concrete; parts of me are numb and others I haven't felt in hours. It would worry me more if I didn't imagine what it might feel like to rip Priscilla's father's throat out with my teeth.

Priscilla hasn't returned since I told her to leave me. I don't blame her, and no matter what my cock thinks, I don't trust her fragile body in my hands right now. If I had her under me, I'd fill every single one of her holes with my seed until she begged for mercy. Then I'd do it again just so she understands who owns her...who she owes.

If I get out of here, I'll make sure she is very aware of the debt between us.

I close my eyes and try to imagine her soft soapy scent. Not the overly perfumed woman from the casino but the delicate woman in leggings who fucked me in her fist even as I growled at her. She was stronger than the woman I met that first night.

Sound comes from the hall. Voices and feet rushing by. It must be a day for a visit or a bath. I lean to sniff myself, but I can't tell what's my stench or the stench of the cell I've been stuck in for fuck knows how many days. They came in with a hose two days ago and washed me down before they sent Priscilla to follow.

Maybe Daddy Dearest doesn't care if I smell for his visit. More thumping boots and voices echo into the room. I don't bother straining to listen. They never talk loud enough to hear unless they stand right outside the heavy steel door.

I won't be here much longer. Either I'll figure out how to get free, or Kai and the others will come for me. We don't leave our own to face capture and torture for long. My friends are probably already hunting for me.

Would they figure out what happened? Check the security tapes in the casino and mark the lovely prostitute who hasn't shown up for her shift since then as the culprit? Not to mention, Kai already knows some things since we spoke on the phone before they took me.

I just have to wait it out and see what happens. It takes time for me to calm the rage boiling under my skin. More time than usual, which should worry me if I didn't fucking care who bears the brunt of it.

The noises outside continue until they grow louder and stop outside my door. Visit, I think. But I didn't think they'd try to talk to me again after I shut them down the last time. As if I'd betray the people I care about, the people I love. Just because they haven't figured out the meaning of loyalty doesn't mean that the concept doesn't exist.

The heavy door slides open, and I blink against the light flickering on. I have to open and close my eyes a few times to let them grow accustomed to the glare overhead.

Arthur Capri saunters in, leaving the guards in the hall, and closes the door at his back. No doubt wanting to mitigate the risk I might escape somehow.

I don't speak to him. If he wants something from me, he can ask me. I won't prompt him or give him some kind of opening he thinks he can manipulate.

The man spins the chair to sit as gracefully as he did the first time we talked. I watch him carefully. One of the best things about everyone assuming you're useful for brute strength and nothing else…they often spill their secrets, thinking I'm too dumb to grasp their significance.

I hope he's dumb enough to give me something I can use to take him down so forcefully that his entire family name is wiped from existence. Doubtful, but I need something to latch on to until I'm free of this hellhole.

His gaze sweeps over me indifferently. "How are you feeling?"

I settle against the cold rock at my back. "I can't wait to rip your legs off like a daddy longlegs when I get out of these restraints."

If my threat scares him, he doesn't even blink. "Graphic, but I expect nothing less from you, at least by what I've seen so far."

"Insulting me won't make me want to prove myself to you. Let's just get on the same page here. Your usual integration and manipulation techniques aren't going to work on me. It won't work on any of the five. You should just know that now to save you some time."

He waves his hand and shifts subtly in the chair. "I have no interest in your friends. I wanted you, and I got you, didn't I?"

"To torture? Did I spit in your cereal or something? I haven't done anything to your little obscure offshoot of the Capri family. Your brother or whatever, and his ilk, I can't say the same for them. Hell, I didn't know you even existed until you decided to show yourself. You could have stayed obscure and off our radar."

Something passes in his eyes, but it's too fast for me to catch. "It would have only been a matter of time before Kai found me. He's relentless when it comes to wrongs perpetrated against him. I knew my days in the shadows were numbered the moment I learned the councilwoman used my drugs on him."

I sigh aloud, letting it echo in the small room. This is why I'm not the brains of our operation. My patience is finite. "What do you want, Capri?"

He blinks, and it's his only sign of discomfort. "I want to know what it will take to make peace between Capri and Doubeck."

"And you thought I'd be the best person to ask? Why not contact Adrian directly?"

"I'm not an idiot. He'd skin me alive before I even said a word, just for knowing my family name. I don't have any illusion that Adrian means to wipe my entire family out of existence and his five plan to help him."

I keep my face slack, neutral, to hide the glee inside me at the thought. "And once again, I ask, why did you choose me for this conversation? I'm neither politically savvy nor beautiful and charming to the ladies. You'd have been better served capturing one of the others."

He shakes his head. "No, if I touched one of the twins, there would have been a firestorm considering what the lovely Andrea has already endured at my family's hands. The others…well… you each have your own weaknesses."

"What's mine?"

The corner of his mouth twists in some sort of macabre smile. "I don't intend to show you my hand so soon, Ivan. Play with me a little longer, and maybe I'll give you a few of my secrets."

He can't be much older than Adrian, but he speaks as if he's eighty. The cadence and verbiage grating in how much they aren't quite right. Not to mention my patience has never been something to boast about.

"So you want me to do what? Talk to Adrian about peace between us? To do that, you're going to have to let me out of here. Then you're going to have to convince me it's worth the effort, considering how you've treated and drugged me for days. Not the best tactic to get someone to speak on your behalf."

Again, he looks completely unconcerned. "No, I'm not worried about that. I have ways to manage if you decide to become unreasonable. Right now, I'd like to attempt a negotiation before I resort to more permanent methods."

I don't even want to know what the fuck he means by that. I shrug, tingles running up my arms into my cramped shoulders. "Then negotiate. You're going to need something I want first, and there's nothing here I want but blood staining my hands."

"There is one thing I can offer you. Something I think you want very badly. For what? I can't say. But she's useless to me, so fuck her, kill her, rip her apart piece by piece if that is your will. I don't personally care about whatever path you take. It'll just mean more cleanup."

I may want to murder every single one of these bastards, but I'm not idiot enough to do it where they can videotape me and use it to their advantage later. "I don't know what you're talking about."

He leans over on his knees, his face now strangely animated, his eyes bright. "My daughter, Ivan. I offer you my daughter in exchange for your vow that you'll speak to Adrian on my behalf."

The door opens behind Arthur, and a guard hauls her into

the room. She's wearing nothing but a skimpy white thong and a matching bra. By the bruises on Cilla's skin, she didn't volunteer for this assignment.

I hate the purple marks against her creamy pale flesh. I jerk at the restraints, no doubt adding fuel to Arthur's belief in my desire for her, but I don't care.

Arthur turns and waves at the guard, who gives Priscilla a shove forward and leaves, the door closing heavily after him.

"Daughter Mine, come here and be reasonable. You do this to keep us all safe. If you don't, well, Ivan's friends are going to firebomb our home out of existence."

I give him a gleeful smile at the idea and let him see how much I want to be the one holding the torch.

Priscilla takes a few steps forward, her long blond hair swinging down her back to swish along her trim waist. It once again highlights the bruises on her skin. I scan up to her face, and rage rushes through me in a white-hot blast.

She has blood dripping down her chin from a split lip and bruises at her temple and on the right side of her face. She's wearing makeup, but I can see the discoloration even in the dim overhead lighting.

Arthur gives her a little push toward me until I can touch her ankles with my feet. I wrap my lower legs around her and tug her closer until my face is almost in line with her belly. Just the scent of her calms the anger spitting and raging through me. Enough that I can think a little bit more clearly. "Who hurt you, Malyshka?"

She whimpers as I lean my forehead into her soft skin. "No one. I'm fine. It was an accident."

The excuse of a woman accustomed to lying to protect herself. To protect others who don't deserve it. "Don't fucking lie to me. Say anything you want. I don't give a shit, but don't fucking lie to me."

She whimpers, and I lean back again so I can look up into her face. Her makeup around her eyes is smudged from tears, and I want to murder everyone all over again.

"Well..." Arthur stands behind Priscilla. "I'll leave you alone to take your payment. Then we shall discuss this deal some more."

He leans close enough that I can almost reach out and grab his skin in my teeth. But he's gone in a heartbeat, and it takes a minute to realize he cut the zip tie holding one of my hands.

I narrow my eyes and let my useless arm flop to my lap. "What the fuck?"

"You can't very well enjoy your prize if you can't touch her, can you?"

11

CILLA

Every part of my body, from my face to my ribs, aches. The guards, angry I wouldn't come along meekly, weren't so gentle when they dragged me out of bed earlier. Hiding under the covers doesn't offer much protection against meaty hands and steel-toe boots.

So here I am, covered in bruises, being offered up like a prize sacrifice to a dragon. A dragon with dragon friends who'd eat us all in a heartbeat.

I keep my eyes averted from where he's shuffling around, no doubt trying to free his other hand from the zip ties. I don't see the point, but then again, I've been the roll-over-and-take-it kind for a while.

Quietly, so I don't alert him to movement, I test the door handle. Those bastards would lock me in, wouldn't they?

It's not enough that they humiliated me when they stripped off my clothes and when they punched and kicked me into submission. They had to make it clear I was nothing more than property to be traded.

The room feels colder than before, or maybe it's the adrenaline crash from my beating.

I risk a peek at him and freeze. He's watching me.

He's angry, but I don't think he'll hurt me. Much. "Are you cold too?"

His eyes narrow to slits, and he gives his hand another jerk. The only way he's getting free is if he breaks something. I don't know enough about him to see if it's his dominant hand or not.

I keep my eyes on him and slide to the floor to sit on the cold concrete. It keeps me out of range of him. Any minute now, he's going to realize he can maneuver enough to grab the chair or the table in the center of the room. If he uses them against me, I have no way to fight back. Maybe he can McGyver a way to cut his other hand loose, and then I'd really be in trouble.

"Hey!" He shouts, and I jump. But he's not looking at me. He's yelling and staring around at the room's corners, hunting for the camera lens. "I didn't agree to your terms. Get her out of here."

I wrap my arms around myself and try to be smaller, insignificant. If I'm not here, I can't be the target of his rage or someone else's.

"I'm not done talking to you, Arthur!" he yells again.

When he's speaking, he scares the shit out of me, but yelling, screaming, he's downright terrifying. Like he's one second away from ripping someone's head off. All I know is I don't want it to be me.

I feel his eyes back on me when no one comes after several minutes. I glance up and brace my chin on my knees. "I'm sorry about this. I don't know when they will come back for me, or you, for that matter."

"What do they want now? What does he want?" His voice is gravel, and I swallow against the way it rakes through me.

I shrug and watch him in the dim light. Since they brought

him here, the room has been mostly dark. Now, with a bit of light casting shadows across his body, I can get a good look at him. "Why are you so calm?" It's been bugging me for days. Why isn't he worried about being stuck here, about dying here?

"Who says I'm calm?"

I wave at his body. "You look calm. Like you're hanging out waiting for something to happen? I know they've been pumping who knows what kind of drugs in you. I can see you're hard right now, so why aren't you climbing up the walls for relief?"

When they load me up with drugs, for whatever test they feel like conducting for the week, I can't resist any of them—from the ones that make me feel like a walking zombie to the ones that make me feel like I'll die if I don't get someone inside me. Of course, there was always a guard or chemist willing to help in any way I might feel the need during these experiments.

I watch him carefully, looking for the same signs I exhibit under the influence, but he's still eerily calm. Like a cobra coiled and ready to strike the second anyone gets close enough. Maybe that's it. He's waiting for someone to inch into his perimeter. Give themselves up to his menace.

His eyes narrow at me again, and I tug my gaze away. I'm not about to be the volunteer mouse to be his next meal. He can't reach me now, but it's only a matter of time before one of the guards comes in to shove me into his arms.

I sweep my eyes around, from the door to him and back to the door. There's nothing here for me to use to protect myself. Nothing here to help me escape. I'm in my underwear, for God's sake. The second I get out of here, I'll be a target to the others. The guards love to play with me, and my father has never stopped them from using me any way they feel.

"What are you looking for?" His voice startles me, and I huddle into myself more.

I don't look at him when I answer, hoping not to provoke

him. "I'm not looking for anything. I'm just sitting here, hoping someone can take me out of here soon."

"Done playing, are we? You've been pleased to come in here to help me for days. Why aren't you in the mood to help me now? Because it's at your father's bidding instead of your own? Do you know how fucked up that is? You only fear me when your father orders you to play damsel? Is that what you're doing now, playing a role so I'll bite and take you as his twisted form of payment?"

I inch into the corner, edging closer to the door even if I can't get outside of it. "I don't know what you mean. I've never wanted any of this."

"You weren't in here offering to ride my dick mere hours ago? What was that? Charity? Or are you playing games with me? Doing your father's bidding and making me think it's all you? That you want to help me out of the kindness of your heart?"

"I—no, it's not like that. I want—wanted to help you. He had nothing to do with it. He didn't even know I'd snuck in." My voice shakes, and I can't keep the tears from sliding down my face. The salt stings the cuts there.

"No, why are you like this? Why did you stay after all this time? Why prostitute yourself when you could run? When you could go anywhere and do anything else?"

A fine thread of anger spools through me, starting in my gut until I'm clenching my hands around my knees. "You don't know shit about my life or why I did what I did. You don't know how many times I tried to get away from him. The last time, he broke my foot and let his guards play with me. The time before that, he kept me drugged for a month, so I couldn't move, couldn't speak, could barely breathe. They had to feed me." I cut off the confession and stare straight again, not letting him get to me. It's what he wants. The second I give in to my anger and go for him, he'll have me in his hands, and I won't be able to free myself.

"Smarter than you look, I see. What else did Daddy Dearest do to you? Call me curious."

I keep my mouth shut and glare straight ahead. He's trying to get to me, and it's working. I hate that it's working. The bastard.

"Should I tell you what my father did to me?"

I swallow, absolutely refusing to respond to him.

"He'd say he did everything he could to turn me into a man. Which included locking a little boy in a closet until he got over his fear of the dark. Locking a little boy in a closet for days at a time until the shadows became his friends. He shot me in the leg to show me what it felt like and to teach me to use a gun. He knifed me in the arm for the same reason. My father was the worst kind of sadist until the day I watched Adrian slit his throat in front of me. I was fifteen."

I keep the questions in my head off my lips. A man like him doesn't have an easy childhood, an easy upbringing. He wears his trauma inked into his skin. But that doesn't mean he didn't turn into the same kind of person his father was. That he doesn't use that pain to hurt others. That's something I'll never be. Something I'll never do.

"Nothing to say to that. It's only the tip of the iceberg, so to speak. I've been hurt in every single way that it's possible to hurt another person. You're not the only one who's had a shitty life. But how you use that pain makes you who you are."

The fissure of anger running through me erupts, and I finally look at him. "You don't know shit about me or about what I've been through. Unlike you, I don't walk around murdering people, selling them, or giving others weapons to do the same. I'm nothing like you, and from where I sit, I'm not the one squandering the gift of being alive."

His eyebrow is raised, a twisted smile on his lips. "You think you're better than me because you don't use your pain to hurt others. Do I have that right? Soon you'll learn it's the best way to use that pain. Hurt the assholes out there determined to kill you or those you love. Use that pain to bring down empires and hobble kingdoms. It's the only safe way to get it out. It's the reason I can sit here calmly because I know your father won't survive this situation. He thinks he can maneuver me, but he will learn a lesson quickly."

I watch him now, and he's not lying. He does look calm. Like he could take down an elephant, but calm with the knowledge that he'd win against it.

I swallow my shame and guilt and rest my chin on my knees again. "It doesn't matter. I'll never get out of here. He'll never let me go free. As long as he's alive, I'll be his prisoner."

There's noise in the hall, and I shift tight to the corner. The door opens, and one of the guards steps in. He's in all black, his usual cargo and button-down uniform. Andre. One of the few guards who's focused on me for some time. The second I'm drugged or forced into anything, he's there, waiting to take advantage of the situation and of me.

"What are you doing?" he asks, staring down at me, his boots only inches from my cold bare feet.

I swallow and tilt my face away in case he might strike out like he did earlier when I wouldn't get out of bed.

"I asked you a question, bitch," he hisses, his voice low and soft.

Ivan speaks from the other side of the room. "Can I help you? She belongs to me right now. If you touch her, I'll kill you." There's so much hatred in his tone. So much promised pain.

Shit. It will only make Andre angry, and then he will use that against me.

I tuck myself down, trying to make myself as small as possible. It's the only way to stay alive.

12

IVAN

The bastard's hands are on her skin, and I'm two seconds from ripping his head from his body. "Don't fucking touch her."

The guard smirks at me and hauls Priscilla to her feet. She lets out a whimper that further ignites my rage.

"Hey, asshole!" I stretch to get closer, up in a crouch, the best I can manage with one hand still pinned. "Let her go. Walk out of the room, or I'm going to fucking obliterate you."

As I expect, he shoves her against the wall and crowds in close, aligning his body with hers. Oh, hell fucking no. "I said, let her go."

When he again ignores me, I call out to Arthur, hoping he doesn't want to risk his precious truce. "Are you going to let him ruin your shot? Because I don't use sloppy seconds. Get him out before you lose a guard."

The man smirks at me. "You think he's watching? No, he's already back in his lab. It's just me now, and I've missed this little piece of ass while she's been hunting you down for us."

Priscilla whimpers and turns her face to the corner while the guard leans in to kiss her.

Something inside me snaps. I jerk my arm, trying to get closer, reach him, get him off her. "Fight him, Malyshka. You belong to me until I say otherwise."

But she only cries, trying to keep her face averted. I struggle harder and reach the table to shove it toward them.

It screeches across the concrete, and the guard blocks it with one hand, releasing a chuckle. "Whooa, almost got me there. Sit tight, I'll be done in a second, and you can have your turn."

I scream at him, "Leave her alone. Don't fucking touch her."

The more I rage, the more the bastard lets his hands roam down her body. When he pinches her nipples, I wrench my arm so hard that something cracks in my shoulder. It doesn't matter. I won't let him have her. Not here. Not now. Not ever.

"Back away," I spit at him. "You don't want to test me on this. I don't know what fucking happened to make you think you can get away with this now, or hell, maybe you've done this before, and you've always been able to get what you want. But not today. Let. Her. Go."

The guard tosses me another look. He doesn't give a shit. Hell, maybe he has no idea who I am or what I'm capable of, but my fingers are already itching to show him exactly what he's too stupid to see. He's waving a red flag in my face, and he's about to find out how much of a mistake he's making.

"Fucking fight, Priscilla. If you don't fight, I'm going to make sure you regret it after I'm done fucking bashing this asshole's skull in. Fight him, baby, or I will do it for you." I keep pulling my hand, my arm, wrenching my shoulder. Nothing loosened.

The guard dips his hand into her underwear, and Priscilla releases a fresh sob, sinking down so the man has to hold her up to keep his hand where he's placed it.

I've had enough. I step back to the wall and eye the zip tie. I can break it, but it'll mean breaking something in my hand or my wrist, and while this hand isn't my dominant hand, I don't like the idea of being vulnerable while I'm stuck here. Plus, I suspect they would use my injury as an opening to load me up with more of their fucked-up drugs.

I take a deep breath and let it out slowly, then I shift my arm and twist my wrist around so the tie cuts into my skin. Blood drips, but I don't stop until the moisture and the angle allow me to slip my hand from the tie.

It falls limp at my side, the feeling slowly returning since I've been able to stand for a while now, restoring blood flow, but it's useless for the moment. It doesn't matter. I don't need two hands to kill this asshole.

He doesn't see me coming. His focus is on Priscilla. But she does. The second she spots me over the man's shoulder, she sinks down, trying to drop out of his grasp to cover her head and keep herself safe. So she can be smart, even if she wasn't willing to fight this asshole.

I grab the man's shoulder and slam him face-first into the wall. He bounces off it, and the rock ensures he comes away with a bloody nose. Hopefully, it's broken.

He swings at me, but I've got more experience than him, so I dodge the punch. It sends him off balance, and I use the opportunity to slam him into the wall once more. Blood sprays in a fan, dotting me and Priscilla, where she's tucked herself into the corner, hugging her knees.

The guard staggers, and I hold the collar of his shirt, but I look at her. "What's his name?"

She blinks, only realizing I'm speaking to her. "A-A-Andre. His name is Andre."

I pat his cheek, my hand finally usable. I flex my fingers and then meet his eyes. "And has Andre pulled this shit before? You get locked in here, and he decides to come in and see if you need a little help with whatever drug you're doped up on that day?"

She whimpers and nods hard, then hides her face again.

"Oh, Andre, I have bad news for you. I always keep my promises. You're about to die, but I want to find out how bad that death will be first. How many times have you visited Cilla here, would you say? Once...?"

His eyes go wide, and I know it's not once. "Twice...five times? Give me a number."

When he doesn't answer, I nudge Cilla's foot with my own. "How many times has this asshole raped you?"

She sobs and then whispers, "I don't know. Too many to count."

Andre sputters. "Whoa, hey now. I never raped her. She always begs me for it."

Wrong fucking answer, asshole. I slam his face into the wall again. It feels good to feel his blood spray fresh again. All over the wall, my hand, my chest. My patience is done, and I continue to slam him face-first into the wall while I scream at him. "If she is drugged out of her mind, she can't beg for it, you fucking prick. That's called rape."

She cries softly, and I can hear each little sob over Andre's muffled groans. I don't stop slamming his face until his body goes limp, and I have to drop him. I let him fall at her feet in a heap, then step over him to get to her.

She's covered in as much blood as I am, but I don't care. I drag her to her feet by the upper arms, back her into the door, and press myself along her body. I want nothing more than to wrap her legs around my hips and fuck her into the steel. It doesn't matter, though, because I won't. Not while I'm drugged, and I don't know if she is. "Why didn't you fight him?" I scream in her face.

She flinches and closes her eyes, turning the same way as him, trying to keep her face safe from my wrath.

"Answer me," I growl.

Again, she says nothing, only sobs, tears making streaks through the blood on her cheeks.

I back away, needing distance before I do something I might regret. If a woman needs to be killed, I don't care if I'm the one to do the job, but I don't want to hurt her. If I keep coming at her in this state, then I will. That's something I can never take back.

I reel around the cell, the walls too tight, too close. There's nowhere to go, no distance to be had.

She sobs, and I pound the walls with my fist. "Stop fucking crying. Stop it. Why the fuck didn't you fight him?"

Another sob, then a sniffle. "He always wins and takes what he wants anyway. It's pointless to fight. I learned that a long time ago. Fighting only leaves you more broken when it's done."

I hit the wall again, feeling the pain up my arm and into my elbow. My wrist is still bleeding, and I'll need to deal with it soon, but first, I need to calm down. We need to get out of here.

I round on her, and she shrinks to the floor in front of the door. It's not enough, though. I stalk back to her, but she crawls through the blood on the floor as if she might get away.

Her handprints dot the concrete on the other side of the pool, and I stalk her to the other side of the room, where I'd been secured. I get around the table and drop to my knees. The ground is cold, but I'm hot and sweating from the adrenaline and the movement. "Are you running from me, Priscilla? You can't escape, so why are you trying to get away?"

She shrugs and rubs her nose with the back of her hand. "I'm not trying to get away from you, just the blood, I guess."

I swipe the tears off her face and the blood as well. "You're a shit liar. Don't worry. I can teach you how to do it right. Now..." I try to keep my voice calm and even. As if she might spook at the slightest inflection. "When did you stop fighting? Did you used to fight them?"

She nods and stares over my shoulder at the wall opposite

the bloody pool. "I used to fight, but then they'd make it worse. Drug me more or make it hurt worse. I learned to just submit, and it'll be over faster. I couldn't stop it, so what the hell was the point?"

I grab the back of her neck and pull her toward me so I can look deep into her eyes. "The point is you die before you make yourself another victim."

She shoves at my chest, but I keep her in my grasp, her scent reaching me over the sharp tang of the blood. "Is that what you did? Fight? You never took the easy road against your father? Never stopped him from hurting you or anyone else?"

"It doesn't matter what I did. I was asking about you. At what point did you give up? Can you even remember? Why let your father play these games with you all this time?"

She sniffles again, and I glance at her full lips, imagining them around my cock. Shit. The drugs. I release her and tuck my hands into my lap.

"If I didn't do what he asked, he threatened to give me to one of my uncles, and then he'd show me what happens to the children that get sent away to them. He thinks he's better than his brothers, more moral, but he's been drugging and using me my entire life. I don't know why. I didn't do anything to deserve it."

I clench my fists and shake my head. "Of course, you didn't, *Malyshka*. Bad men are just bad men. They don't need an excuse to do evil. I do bad things every single day, and most of the time, it's because someone just pisses me off enough that I explode."

She stares at me, her eyes searching mine. "But you've been kind to me. Nice, I guess, in your own sort of weird way. I don't think you're evil."

I cup her chin, unable to resist the temptation of touching her again. "Don't misunderstand, Cilla. I'm a very bad man. And I don't intend to release you anytime soon."

13

CILLA

I should be terrified of him. My body screams at me to get away, run, and hide. But the parts that have conditioned me to cower, lie down, and die won't allow me to move. Not under the heavy weight of his hold or his eyes. "I..." My voice shakes, and my shame is a hot wash through me on top of everything else.

There might yet be a part of me that can feel shame, at least when he's staring at me so intently; it's like he can see inside to my deepest, darkest thoughts. The very ones keeping my body hostage in his brutal grip.

"I...I...I..." he mocks me, but there's no vehemence in it. Like I'm a child he's trying to teach a lesson in the most sadistic way possible. "Finish what you were going to say, but you better fucking make it good."

I shake my head. "I don't know what you want me to say. I can't just be a different person in the five minutes I've known you." There it is. The hot shame is covered in an icy blanket of anger. The bastard thinks he knows me. That he knows a single thing about my life or why I am the way I am. "You don't know shit about me, so if you're going to escape, please, be my guest. You don't have to make me feel like shit on the way out the door."

He narrows his eyes, and the tiniest smile flicks at the corner of his mouth. Barely there and gone just as quickly. "That's what I'm waiting for, Malyshka. I want your anger. Your rage. I want to feel it on my skin as you rip these bastards to shreds."

My hands are shaking as he tugs me toward him slowly. His voice is barely a whisper now. "I want your rage and, if need be, your willingness to die as you take your enemies down."

"But that's not who I am. I don't murder or hurt people. No matter how many times I've been hurt myself." Of course, someone like him wouldn't be able to see that or understand it.

His face shifts, the snarl out of his mouth making me flinch back to safety. "What the fuck is wrong with you that you can't hurt those who hurt you? I didn't tell you to go find an innocent." He kicks the corpse on the floor, but I keep my eyes firmly on him. "He would kill you no matter what. Hell, he was probably planning to one day kill you while he raped you. This man had death in his eyes, and you were just going to roll over and let him do it?" The last is snarled in my face, his breath hot on my skin.

I turn my face to the side to stay out of range of a strike, but he won't have me retreating from him. Everyone else, he wants me to fight, but not him. His hands come around my waist, and I shove at his chest. "No. Didn't you just give me that little pep talk of death, telling me to fight? This right here…is me fighting."

He chuckles for real this time. But it's dark and deadly. "You can fight all you want, Priscilla. In fact, please do. I'll take pleasure when you submit to me once and for all. The moment all the fight leaves your body, all the anger, all the fear, and you give yourself over to me. That is what I'm waiting for. So tell me, what are you waiting for?"

Tears thread hot and wet through the already flaking blood on my face. He'd wiped some of it off, but I still felt covered in it. I can only shake my head again. "I don't know what I'm waiting for. I guess...for the pain to finally end. I just want one day when I'm not humiliated or hurt to please someone else. One day."

He pulls me to my feet gently as I wobble on unsteady legs. "Come here."

It occurs to me that guards will be coming at any moment. That we need to make a run for it while we can. Or maybe he can make a run for it while I distract whoever comes to check on things.

I open my mouth to suggest that plan, but he buries his face into the side of my neck, making me squeak before I can even get a word out. His nose grinds into my muscle, not hard enough to hurt, but enough to let me know he's there. When his hand cups the back of my head, I let my eyes close and breathe. I can't smell him. Nothing but the sharp metallic bite of blood, but something in me calms, loosens, and relaxes as he cradles the nape of my neck.

He takes a few breaths, then lifts his face away to stare down at me. "Now that we can think more clearly, tell me about the guards."

I'm curious about what the fuck just happened, but I can't bring myself to ask why his breathing against my neck settled us both down. "There are usually only a couple on duty at a time. One to guard this area, one to switch off sporadically. There also might be some outside the lab. I don't know." It's been a long time since I memorized all of the guards' schedules. I've been preoccupied with the ones guarding Ivan's cell.

He only nods and stares off at the wall behind me for a moment. "Let's get out of here first, and then we can figure everything else out."

Lightning fast, he turns to grab the legs of the dead guard

and strips his boots, pants, and shirt in seconds. I barely have time to gape when he puts them on himself and digs into the pocket for the keys. "Let's get the hell out of here before I do something I'll regret."

There's not enough time for me to ask questions. He's already tucking my hand into his and leading me over the body toward the door. Then we are in the hall, and everything seems to snap up around me like a high-speed chase.

We are running through the hall, and he looks at me for a second. "Underground, right?"

I only nod and clutch his hand tighter in my own. If we get separated, he'll leave me, and I'll be dead within hours. My father doesn't take failure well. The long hallway is empty, and we race toward cinder block walls through the maze of my father's underground labs. It's extensive. Even I haven't been through some of it. And he delights in showing me off to his friends.

He's panting in front of me. Despite all those muscles, days of drugs, minimal food, and water wore him down. I try to ignore the pang of guilt in my chest. "Fuck." His voice is barely audible against the clap of our feet on the painted concrete floors. "I'd give my left nut for a goddamn stairwell right about now."

We keep running, and it's like a funhouse. I should have led him back the way I knew toward my room. But we'd have been trapped at the end, where the guards stay between shifts. No telling how many might be here sleeping.

There's a door up ahead, and I squeeze his hand and point. His shoulders seem to relax as we race toward it, only to stop two feet from the knob, with a guard who just rounded the corner staring open-mouthed.

Ivan drops my hand and steps forward. I'm behind him and can feel the menace rolling off him. The guard falters backward for a moment, and it's exactly the opening Ivan needs to slam him against the cinderblock wall hard enough to knock him out.

Ivan lets the man slide to the floor and then braces his hand on the wall while he breathes heavily for a moment. Shit. Is he going to make it?

His eyes slide to mine, his pupils pinpoints in the bright light after being caged in darkness for days.

He takes my hand again, deliberately wrapping his fingers through mine, and leads me toward the door. "Are you ready to get the hell out of here?"

I can only nod, my heart so high up my throat that he has to see it in my eyes.

The door, thankfully, isn't locked. It opens quietly, and we step into a stairwell. Ivan grabs the door so it closes softly, then creeps to the banister to look up. We are on the bottom floor, and it won't be long before someone notices our disappearance.

He turns and places his finger over his lips. Quiet. I can do quiet. I nod and let him lead me silently up the flights of stairs. He stops at a couple of doors to peek into the small window.

On the third set of stairs, we stop again, and this time, he slowly opens the door and tugs me through, releasing my hand so I can go in front of him. "Stay quiet and right beside me. We have to be quick about this."

I nod and wait for him to lead. He wraps his hand around my waist and bends so we are both stooped, creeping through a garage I didn't even know existed. Every time I leave the house, a car is brought to the front door for me. But I guess it makes sense with so many people working here they'd need a place to put the cars.

Lost in thought, I stumble, but his arms are under my elbow, and he keeps me upright and moving until we stop next to a beat-up Mercury of some kind. "This is the one you want to steal?"

He tugs me to the driver's side and bends down to the lock. With the keys he took from the guard, he waves a key that looks exactly like a house key. Weird.

It fits into the lock perfectly, and I stare open-mouthed. "Really? How the hell did you know this was his car?"

"Cheap shoes, cheap clothes, asshole. He doesn't give a shit about his possessions. I just needed to find the worst fucking car in the garage." He shoves me in first, and it takes some maneuvering over the console.

He settles in the driver's seat and quietly closes the door. The car smells like sweaty socks and stale pizza, just like the guard. I cover my mouth as the scent assaults me all over again. The memories threaten to rise up along with the last meal I ate.

"Keep it fucking together, got that?" His voice is sharp, and I manage to meet his eyes and nod.

He slips the key into the ignition, and the car fires to life. I hold my breath as he pulls away. Any moment, someone is going to stop us, right? Come after us? This feels like it's too easy, and for me, when things are too good to be true, I learn pretty quickly to regret getting involved.

We pull out of the spot, and he maneuvers us toward the ramps leading up to the street.

Of course, there's a guard with some kind of weapon across his chest. He's big and beefy, and I've never seen him before. Maybe he's a separate outside kind of guard.

I huddle into the seat, and Ivan reaches back to grab a towel to throw over me. It covers me, and I gag at the scent of the bastard who owned it.

Ivan talks for a moment, low and insistent, but I can't make out the words when everything inside me is screaming under the towel.

The second I hear the handle stop from his manually rolling

up the window, I chuck the towel to the floor and kick it as far away as possible.

I gag one more time, and Ivan wraps his hand around the back of my neck and squeezes. "Settle, *Malyshka*. It's almost over."

14

IVAN

I keep my eyes on the rearview mirror and don't bother stopping my hands from running up her thigh.

She glances down but doesn't react as I stall my hand mid-thigh and leave it there.

My nerves are shredded, and the fresh batch of drugs raging through me isn't helping the adrenaline now slowly leaking out of me. I can't think straight. The only thing in my head is getting inside her wet heat and losing myself.

I give her thigh a slight squeeze, using the softness of her skin to ground myself and pull me back from the edge. "We're almost there."

Her eyes dart to my face, and I keep my gaze bouncing from her, the road, and the rearview mirror. So far, no one is coming after us. It might not occur to them to track the cars of their employees. But I'd bet a lot of money that Cilla has some kind of tracker in her body. Her father is just bastard enough to want complete control over her life.

Adrian placed a tracker in Valentina, but it was to keep her safe. If Cilla has something, it's all about fear and control, not safety and love.

"Where are we going?" Her voice is thin and quiet.

I turn slightly to see her eyes before facing the windshield again. "Did they give you more drugs before they shoved you into my cell?" I cup the back of her neck with the hand I had on her thigh.

Cilla shakes her head.

"Are you sure? They didn't give you anything? Do you know if they placed a tracker in you? Something we need to remove before we're safe?"

She jumps, and I squeeze the back of her neck a little tighter.

"It's okay. Calm down. If there is a tracker, I'll take care of it."

"I don't like the fact that I don't know. That they could have done something to me while I was unconscious or under the influence of whatever my father gave me. You can remove it if there's something inside me?"

I gently squeeze the back of her neck and keep my eyes locked on the little cul-de-sac streets until I spot the ones I'm hunting for. The suburbs make great places for safe houses, and this one, in particular, is perfect so I can dump this shitbag car in the nearby lake. Kai and I worked out a plan ages ago, just in case anyone needed to get rid of a vehicle quickly.

She's shaking, and I release her only long enough to flip on the heat. The adrenaline must be crashing for her too, and she's wearing little more than scraps of lace they'd forced her into to tempt me. They work, hell, she can just be standing in front of me breathing, and I'd pop a boner. She doesn't need fancy lace or lingerie. Considering our circumstances, I'm hoping these thoughts are a side-effect of the drugs and nothing more. I don't need a complication like her in my life.

I'll get her to safety and set her up, but then I'm putting some distance between us while I hunt her father down like a rabid dog.

I pull up outside a little bungalow, put the car in park, and cut the engine. It takes a second to scan the mirrors, looking for any neighbors outside. I might be ignorable, but a half-naked blonde isn't going to hide easily.

"Ready?" I whisper, grasping the door handle.

She grabs her door, bracing to shove it open. "Ready for what?"

I push the door and race toward the front of the house. She follows, close on my heels. It takes a few seconds to find the hidden key and unlock the door. I release a slow sigh once we are locked inside.

She takes a few short steps forward, surveying the house. It's been meticulously kept and repaired. We keep all our safe houses stocked and ready to go. Kai even hired a housekeeper to remove the unused food each week and donate it to the local shelter before it goes bad. I couldn't care less about it, but it seems important to him, so no one puts up a fuss.

I watch her explore the small living room. "Where are we?"

It takes effort to drag my eyes off the curve of her back, the way it leads into the fuckable full globes of her ass. "It's a safe house. Don't worry. I won't let them capture you or me again."

She turns to face me, her shoulders squared, chin high. "I need you to make sure they don't have some kind of tracker in me. Do whatever you need to do, but if there's something they can use to find me, I want it out now. Right now."

I stalk to the kitchen, mostly for the distance, and grab a burner phone from the drawer. "In a minute. Right now, I need to check in and get rid of the car." I point at her, the phone curled in my fingers. "You stay here. Don't make me chase you today. You won't like what happens."

Her eyes stretch wide, but she nods and wraps her arms

around her waist. "I'm going to see if I can find something to wear."

I resist getting one last look at her bare skin and leave the house, locking the door behind me.

The street is still empty as I climb into the car and head toward the lake. It's getting dark, and thankfully no one is in the adjacent park. I park on the bank and work up the nerve to drive the vehicle into the water, it'll take a minute to get out of the car, and there's always a chance I won't make it.

I open the door, drop the phone on the bank of the lake, then slam the door shut. It only takes a minute to drive into the water and another to slither out of the window, the frame scraping and bruising my arms and shoulders as I work my way out of it.

When I make it back to shore, I snap up the phone and leave. If anyone sees the car sinking, I don't want them to see me alongside it.

The trek back to the house is harder than our escape. My muscles are screaming, and all of my blood seems to be drained to my cock. Rationally, I know it's the drugs and the days of captivity, but it only fuels my rage, driving it higher the closer I get to the house.

As I walk up the street, trying to look inconspicuous in my blood-stained clothes, I snap open the phone and send a coded text to Kai. No doubt they are all hunting for me. Now he knows I'm alive, which safe house we are holed up in, and when I'll check back in with him again. I need to ensure no one follows us before we go to the penthouse. The Doubeck epicenter isn't a secret, but I won't bring a threat to our doors. Not when I can deal with it on my own.

I twist the phone in my hands and drop the pieces in some overgrown grass as I approach the final turn up the quiet street. It takes a minute to get to the door and check the neighboring houses for onlookers before I go inside. No one seems to be out, thankfully.

I slip inside and lock the handle lock, the deadbolt, and the chain that is usually left unlocked. It won't keep out a determined intruder, but it'll give me enough notice to grab a gun and take care of things before someone reaches us.

Turning to face the living room, I pause. It's empty. Everything neat and tidy, just as it was the moment we arrived. Most importantly, she's not here, and though I didn't specify where she could go, I assumed she would stay put.

The rage I'd been stoking slowly on my walk surges up like a wildfire, and I stalk toward the bedroom in the back of the house. It's also empty. As is the bathroom, the kitchen, and the small supply room that takes up the second bedroom. "Priscilla. You better fucking be here, or we are going to have fucking problems!"

There's no answer, and I start throwing open closets, flipping up the edge of the bedding, and then I have to take a second to curtail my rage before I destroy the place before I've taken a decent shower.

I head back into the kitchen, open the laptop on the counter containing the cameras inside and outside the house, and rewind the footage. I spot Cilla as she heads into the bedroom, but she never comes back out. She couldn't have climbed out the window, right? Why would she when she could walk right out the front door?

Slamming the laptop shut, I go back to the bedroom and scan the space. It still looks the same, except the curtains are pulled tight, keeping the room dark. I flip on the bedside lamp and spot the discarded underwear she'd been wearing near the dresser.

It takes me a minute to track the smudges of her footprints on the carpet leading into the closet. I slam open the door and spot her cowering in the far corner, her legs tucked up in front of her, arms wrapped around them.

"I know I didn't specify where you could go, but I didn't think I'd have to search high and low for you?"

She shakes from her hiding spot. " I told you I was going to find some clothes."

I narrow my eyes and bear down on her. At least she isn't cowering from me. If anything, she's scared of her father and his guards. I squat in front of her, my borrowed uniform cutting into my legs. "Watch the fucking attitude. I don't appreciate being spoken to that way after I saved your fucking life. Even though you didn't deserve it."

She blinks at me, eyes wide. "So we're back to that? Are you going to punish me too? You don't think I've been through enough?"

I snap out my hand and grab her chin hard, then pull her face toward me, her head skimming the bottom of the dress shirts she cowers under. "I'll say when it's enough. Until then, you'll listen to what I say and do it without question."

Her eyes narrow, but she doesn't say anything or pull away.

I lean forward until our lips almost touch and whisper, "Good girl. Now, let me see if you have a tracker, so we can get some undisturbed rest."

She scrambles to her feet, more desperate than I am to check her over. We head into the kitchen, and I grab the RFID scanner from the drawer used for this purpose. I scan her body head to toe, and the scanner blips on the soft undercurve of her right tit.

"Fuck," she breathes.

I kneel and shove the oversized white T-shirt up into her hands so she can hold it. There's a tiny scar on the bottom of her full breast. She wouldn't even notice it as she likely can't see it from her angle. "I have to cut it out."

Gently, I cup her soft flesh, focusing on my task, despite my raging hard-on. There's a tiny lump right under the skin. It'll sting to remove but it shouldn't be too bad. There are worse places to find something like this.

I stand, grabbing the first-aid kit and a sharp knife.

She sits at the table while I lay out the supplies. "Just do it quickly."

I kneel beside the chair, my face almost even with the small lump. "This is going to sting. You going to pass out on me?"

Her look of annoyance is enough to urge me on. I quickly make a shallow cut and use a pair of tweezers to remove the tiny tracker. It's tiny, smaller than I've ever seen. I bandage the cut and then flush the tracker down the toilet while she hopefully puts clothes between her bare skin and mine. Another second, and I might not be able to control what happens.

15

CILLA

They put something inside me. I never knew it was there. How did I not know? Not feel it under my skin, lurking like a time bomb waiting to sink me. I tug my shirt to cover my borrowed boxer briefs and bare skin. Tears pour down my cheeks, and I can't stop them. It's as if they bubble up inside me from the never-ending well of anger, fear, and betrayal.

What did I do to deserve this life? I'm sobbing, the sounds loud and jagged to my ears. A tiny voice tells me to pull myself together, to suck it up because I'm not safe yet. It doesn't matter. I'm in no shape to listen to anyone at the moment. I can barely stand upright, my thoughts messy as I lean my side against the counter.

A hand grabs my chin, and I strike out without thinking of knocking the grasp away. I can't see through my tears, only his dark shape. Rationally, I know it's Ivan, but the thought of letting anyone touch me right now sickens me. My stomach roils, threatening to throw up nothing but bile.

The grip on my chin doesn't loosen, and I blink against the blur of the tears and glare up at him. "Let me go."

He kneels in one smooth move even though his body has to be more battered than mine, having been chained to a wall for several days. "Watch the way you speak to me, Malyshka. You'd hate it if I decide you're not worth keeping alive."

I stiffen and continue glaring. "So you're just like the rest of them, then? Considering me nothing more than an easy distraction? A means to an end? Something to be tossed out with the trash." I swipe at my eyes and nose. "Good to know."

His hold tightens enough to make me try to pull back from him. But he won't let me go that easily. His arm comes around my waist, and he hauls me into his arms in one strike, standing as he does so. I bring my hands up to claw at him and force him to let me go. Force him to see me as a person, even if it's the moment before I die.

I don't realize we're moving until we've reached the bedroom, and we fall onto the bed, with me underneath him. His weight presses me deep, covering every inch possible with his heavy form. "Stop fucking fighting me, Priscilla. I'm not the kind to give in easily, and the more you fight, the more I'll make it hurt as I force you to work for it. Fucking stop it."

I don't freeze, even though some long dormant self-preservation instinct whispers at me to give in, to go limp, let him have his way. Yet I'm tired of letting everyone walk all over me, to let them take more and more and more of me until there's nothing left. I shove at his chest, trying to get him off, but he feels like he weighs a ton, and I don't have a chance.

When I give up shoving at his chest, he wraps his hands around my wrists, stilling them, his entire weight pressing down on my chest and belly. "I'm not fucking them, Cilla!" he roars in my face, and I squeeze my eyes shut, turning my face away as if I might protect it from a blow.

But he doesn't hit me. "Look at me. Now."

I swallow, going still, keeping my eyes closed, face up. When

I don't respond, he seems to press into me harder, somehow forcing the air out of my body. "Fucking look at me," he hisses.

He moves, and then his teeth clamp around the side of my neck hard enough that I whimper. It's not a move to cause pain. And it doesn't. Some twisted part in my body and mind takes it completely differently, shooting a warm heat under my skin.

He eases and releases me, leaving me cold, shivering with the adrenaline and the lost heat of him. "I said I'm not fucking them. You know I'm not them. So why are you acting like I'm going to use you and throw you away like those fucking bastards?"

I hear a drawer slide open, then close. When I open my eyes, I catch his back as he enters the bathroom and slams the door hard behind him.

Some noises leak out of the bathroom. Water running, and I try not to imagine every inch of his sleek, tattooed muscles under hot water. I can't figure out what I'm feeling. Some mixed-up, braided, screwed-up mix of fear, arousal, and shame. The fact that he saw me break down when he was the one that was held captive, the one I helped capture even. I did that to him, and he still treats me better than my father and his men.

I arch up, my muscles protesting, as I sit and stare around the room. It's sparse and decorated with the necessary furniture in beige and gray tones. Like a middle-class hotel room. Nothing personal. Nothing I can use to identify where we are in the city, no way to see if there is anything here that can help me get free and stay free.

The skin on the side of my boob aches, and it hurts to take a full breath. Damn him, damn them all for putting me in this position in the first place. Fucking men who think they can use and abuse us to get what they want.

I scoot to the edge of the bed and stand. The noise in the bathroom doesn't pause, so I creep toward the door and listen for a few minutes. He doesn't burst out, and I'm not brave enough to go inside, so I stay there and press my ear to the painted wood. When the water shuts off, I jump away from the door and scramble back to the bed, over the other side, to make it to the corner.

I don't know how much time has passed. There's only my racing heartbeat to keep track. I stay with my back to the corner and draw my knees up under my T-shirt to stay warm. Nothing happens, though, and soon the pounding in my head slows, and I can breathe again.

Although, as more time passes, I start to get worried. He doesn't exit the bathroom, nor do I hear anything from this side of the door. Eventually, I pry myself out of the corner and approach, listening. It takes a second to get the courage, but I knock softly and wait.

He doesn't answer, and I assume maybe he needs space. Something I understand intimately and am willing to give him. I head into the kitchen and poke around, looking for food. I can't help but smile when I see the fully stocked fridge. Vegetables, eggs, fruit. It looks like someone went to the grocery store yesterday and filled it up.

I pull out the eggs, butter, cheese, and some peppers. There aren't many things I can cook, but eggs are easy enough. Plus, they are cheap. So when things were dire at home, and I had to scrounge around for food, eggs always fit the bill.

The act of cooking relaxes me a bit. Letting me resettle and uncoil my muscles. Everything aches from the running, the adrenaline, all of it. I focus on making myself breathe and relax and finally let myself consider what I can do next.

I make enough food to fill a plate for both of us. No doubt he's dying for food. My father's hospitality was always lacking when it came to his prisoners. If given the choice, I wouldn't eat either, considering how often my father tended to drug people that way. It's easier than resorting to needles or shoving pills down a grown man's throat. Letting him starve and waving food under his nose is much easier.

When he doesn't come out at the scent of food, I dig into my own, letting the flavors chase away the rest of my fear. The doors are locked, and Ivan is in the other room. If anyone shows up, he won't let anyone get to me. If only because he wants to get his revenge on me. It's not ideal, but it's something I can live with for now. At least until a better option presents itself.

I finish up my meal, wash the dishes, and take his food to the bathroom. Should I knock again or try to open it?

I grip the knob but don't dare to intrude, so I put the plate on the floor by the door, hoping he doesn't charge out and get a foot full of eggs. That would suck.

The food is making me heavy and sleepy. So I grab the bedspread and a pillow to take into the closet with me. No doubt he'll drag me back out again, but maybe I can get some sleep before he does.

I curl up with the covers, pulling them up to my chin, my back to the wall in the very farthest corner. It won't help if someone has a gun, but it might take a minute for someone to see me down here, covered up. It's as safe as I can get right now.

Tomorrow I can try to figure out a plan. Maybe I'll get lucky and can make a run for it before he decides to end his vigil in the bathroom. Give myself a head start before he chases me down as promised.

16

IVAN

I blink my eyes open into the blinding light. Everything is too bright, too loud. I reach to rub my eyes, and one knuckle scrapes across my eyelids, but the other…

The noise of handcuffs wakes me, sending me headlong into the nightmares I had about being locked in a hole, chained to a wall, unable to move or defend myself. On the heels of the horror comes the anger, sparking bright hot, and I have to take a minute to try to calm myself down again. The night returns, and my aching balls and the fact that I handcuffed myself to the shower rail, so I didn't go to her come back.

I scrub my free hand up my face. "Fuck…"

My heart is hammering into my ribs. It feels like I'm still there, locked away in Arthur's stupid cage. My dick is still hard, and I still want her, but I think I'll be able to control myself. *Maybe.* I'll stay here for now, at least until I can't feel my pulse in my erection quite so strongly.

Faint light streams in from the frosted glass above my head. It has to be early. My watch was lost when they captured me but years of rising early tell me it can't be later than seven a.m. My mind strays to her. Did she sleep well? Or at all? I wouldn't blame her if she didn't. After the life she's led, nightmares must be a constant companion.

My stomach lets out a soft growl, reminding me it's been days since I've had a full, non-drugged meal.

As long as she's not standing out there naked, it might be fine to risk seeing her, at least long enough to grab something to eat. I need real food. My stomach growls loudly once more.

I catch the sound of something shuffling outside the door, and then she practically falls into the room, a fork in her hand. My eyes catch her bare legs and rake up her body to her breasts, jiggling in the T-shirt, her nipples peaked at the fabric.

My erection rages tighter and the drugged urge to sink into her makes my skin tight. "You have to get out of here."

She stares, her gaze hopping from my tented boxer briefs to me on the floor next to the bathtub, up to my hand secured to the rail. "What the fuck are you doing? You didn't have enough of being restrained by my father?"

I narrow my eyes at her. "You come in here just to bitch at me, or what?"

Her face flashes pink. "No, of course not."

I let the anger roll over me, making no move to squash it down. "Then what the fuck do you want? If you have to pee, go ahead, but there's another bathroom off the guest room if that makes you feel more comfortable."

A tiny line forms between her eyebrows as she scowls my way. "I already found that bathroom, thank you. I was worried about you."

Some of the anger stacked tight in my chest fizzles. "Worried about me?"

She slinks back as if only now realizing how close to danger she might be. "Yes, you came in here last night and never came back out..."

My blood is pounding in my cock, and I squeeze my eyes closed to breathe a moment. I'm in control of my body; it does not control me.

I repeat it several times in my head, then look up at her again. "You should get out. I've reached my limit, and it's not safe for you to be around me right now."

She retreats to the doorway but lingers. "You don't scare me, you know."

Whatever she sees in my face at her statement sends her back another couple of paces. I lean into the wall, resettling despite every position being uncomfortable. "Brave girl to say so when I'm restrained. You feared me a few days ago. Don't mistake self-preservation for affection. I'd do a lot of things to stay alive."

Her hand creeps up her chest to her neck, drawing my eyes until it lays flat between her collarbones. The fear still on her face despite her words. "I'm not an idiot. I'd never think you might be capable of something as soft as affection."

Fuck. Just looking at her is making me harder. But she could be any woman. Any hole to bend over a bed and fuck raw. At least, that is what I'm telling myself. Disgusted by my uncertainty, I narrow my eyes and pin her with a look that has made grown men piss themselves. "Get the hell out, and don't come back unless I call for you."

Thankfully, she doesn't argue. She steps backward and gently closes the door between us.

Something inside me rages at the distance, and not being able to look at her, but it's for the best. I can't wrap my head around her. I want to mark her, dig my fingers in so she bears my bruises, my teeth marks, the scent of my body on her skin. All of which might break her after what she's been through. She's strong, but my body has been a battleground for days, and I don't trust myself not to hurt her like this: straddling the line between sanity and psychosis.

I close my eyes and lean my head back against the wall. I might lose it completely if these drugs don't wear off soon.

The scent of cooking food, bacon, maybe, reaches me a few minutes later and ignites another kind of hunger. One that I'm already fighting. Still, I don't trust myself to leave this room and eat without taking her—claiming her.

I don't know how much time passes, five minutes, five years, but the door opens again, and she steps into the room. Her face is pink and freshly scrubbed, tendrils of the blond hair around her face darker from the water. But my eyes lock on the tray in her hands. "I said to stay the fuck out of here. Don't you listen?"

She purses her lips but says nothing, instead creeping closer. Part of me wants to teach her a lesson and make sure she learns not to fucking disobey my orders, but my stomach shames me, letting out a loud gurgle between us. I drop my eyes and glare at the white shower wall beside me. At least long enough to wrestle with the threads of control I have left.

As she comes closer, she rises up onto her tiptoes like she might bolt for the door at my slightest movement. "I brought you something to eat. I'm sure you're hungry since you haven't eaten anything since last night."

I clench my fists on my thighs. "It's not your job to take care of me. If I want food, I'll get myself fucking food."

The look she gives me is all annoyance. "Is that right?" My stomach chooses right then to growl again. "Your stomach disagrees with you. Very loudly, I might add." I'm close to snapping but somehow manage to keep it together. "Here." She sets the tray on the floor near my curled knee.

It's not pride that keeps me from eating. The memory of Arthur, of the guards, forcing their drugged food down my throat rises up, and I can't force myself to reach out to the tray and eat, no matter how badly I want to.

She clears her throat and swallows loud enough that I can hear it. Which means she's much closer to me than she should be. "If you're still having problems. With the drugs. I can help. It doesn't mean anything. Maybe even just payment for saving me when you saved yourself. Either way, you should let me help you."

I squeeze my fists tight, focusing on breathing through my mouth so I can ignore both her body's clean soapy scent and the food's heady richness. "I told you not to fucking come back in here, didn't I?" My voice is so deep that I don't even recognize it.

Her T-shirt rustles as she shifts closer, sitting up on her calves. "Well, you already know how good of a listener I am. Let me do this. I owe you."

I drop my gaze to her nipples, poking invitingly from the white cotton of the T-shirt. I can even see the pink shadow of her nipples beneath the fabric. Fucking hell. I unclench my fist and press the heel of my palm against the top of my erection, trying to ease some of the ache.

Her hand trails up my thigh to the edge of my boxer briefs, and I almost jump out of my skin. I snatch her wrist, squeezing, feeling her delicate bones in my grasp.

When she doesn't jerk her arm free, I tighten my grip, squeezing enough that she can feel how close to the edge I am. "I said get the fuck out and don't come back."

I release her, but the brat still doesn't listen. Instead, she rises up on her knees, spreads her thighs, and straddles my own thighs. My hips rise up involuntarily, and I slam my free hand on the tile to hold myself back against the wall. "What the fuck do you think you're doing?"

She looks me in the eye, with us almost even, and reaches down to grab my aching cock through my underwear. "Despite people dubbing you the animal, I know you're not stupid. Now let me help you."

I hiss through my nose, closing my eyes to block out the sight of her in my lap. "You have no fucking idea how close I am to snapping. If you touch me, I will hurt you. I promise."

She leans and brushes her lips along my stubbed jaw. Her skin is so soft against mine. "Then hurt me. Use me. Fuck me the way you need to fuck me. I can take it."

My hand strays up to wrap around the back of her ass of its own volition. I stare down at her again, my jaw aching from clenching it so hard. "I'm not like them. When I take you, I want you soaked for me. Screaming. Writhing. I want you spread open like a hero's feast waiting for me to take my fill."

Her eyes grow rounder as I speak, but the gentle tilt of her hips toward me—against me—threatens to be my undoing.

She swallows loudly. "Then do that. Do whatever you want or need to."

I fist her borrowed boxer briefs in my hand, squeezing the material hard enough to rip it. "Not like this. Not while you're drugged, and I'm drugged. Not while I'm fighting for every bit of my control. I'm not like them."

She folds her hand around mine and eases it carefully to the front of her body. I hiss out another breath as my fingers brush the heat of her. Even through the underwear, she's warm and wet. Touching her is like sticking my hand into the flames of fire and expecting not to get burnt. I know the outcome, yet I'm still tempted to do it.

"I'm not drugged. I have a high tolerance, thanks to their testing. All the drugs left my system last night. You don't have to be afraid to hurt me. I can take it. I'm a big girl. Let me make the choice myself. Now touch me." A moment passes, and then another. I can see how much she wants this, how much she cares. It's etched into her features. "Let me do this for you," she adds. The very last frays of my control are in danger of snapping. Her scent makes me rock my hips up toward her, despite my threats, my words telling her to leave me alone to my misery.

I cup my hand underneath her so my fingers can splay wide and let me hold all of her pussy in my hand. "You have no idea what you are unleashing. If you don't leave now, I'm going to hurt you, and I'm going to fucking enjoy every second of it."

She leans in so her mouth brushes against mine in barely a whisper. "Then hurt me if that's what you need. Hurt me until I scream for you."

17
CILLA

Part of me feels guilty for pushing him right now. I should climb off his lap and get out of here, especially with him so close to the edge. But I can't bring myself to let go of him. After all the back and forth we've had for the past week...I'm tired of waiting. Bonus, if it helps him take some of the edge off, then we both get what we need right now.

"Come on," I lean in and whisper the words against his lips.

He doesn't let me pull back, instead snapping his free hand up to the back of my neck to hold me in place while he takes my mouth. Fucking hell. He kisses like he does everything else. Full tilt and then some. His teeth scrape against mine, his tongue tangling, and his hand flexing so his fingers dig into my scalp. Heat pours through me as I straddle his cock right where I want it, lighting up my nerve endings even though two pieces of fabric separate our bare skin.

He rocks up into me with each tiny tilt I give him back, making me feel powerful to have this man under me. I doubt he'll let me stay this way for long, so I'll savor it while I have the chance.

When he pulls his mouth from mine, it's swollen and wet. I can't help but stare at his lips and imagine what they will feel like in other places.

Like he can read my mind, he pulls my face into his shoulder and trails his mouth down the curve of my neck to leave a bite. Pain and pleasure zip through me at once, and I wiggle in his grasp, needing less and more at the same time.

I realize he's stopped moving, so I lift my face, and he allows it, giving me space in his grip. "What's wrong?"

"Reach down and pull my underwear off. Then yours."

I can't help but glance down between us. Where he's hard between my thighs, and I've left a little wet spot on him. I don't have the modesty to be embarrassed anymore.

I wiggle back onto his muscular thighs, grab his underwear, and tug them off his legs. Then I stand and let him get a good look while I remove the clothing I'm wearing too. When I'm completely naked, I climb back across his lap, and he cups his arm around the back of my waist.

He stares down at my breasts, my nipples already tight. "Perfect."

While he looks at me, I get a good look at him. He's long and thick. Bigger than I usually like, but I bet every inch will feel good inside me. He's thicker at the head and tapers down the shaft.

When I try to grab him, he stops my hand before I can touch. "Don't. Use your mouth."

Some women hate giving head, but I love it. Even when they are rough and brutal. There's a power in it that so many people don't see for themselves.

I wiggle down his legs again so my ass is almost resting on his knees. This puts me at eye level with this cock, and I lick my lips. Before he can change his mind, I pull my hair to my right shoulder, drop down, and suck the already beading tip of him into my mouth.

His hips jerk up as he hisses out a breath. "Easy, Malyshka."

I start slow, using my left hand to chase my mouth with every pass as I slowly work him faster and faster. He raises his hips to meet me until he's so deep in my throat I gag.

He grabs the top of my hair in a tight fist. "Don't stop until I tell you to."

The sting on my scalp only makes me wetter as he raises his hips to fuck into my mouth harder and harder. Tears pour down my cheeks, but I fucking love it. The salty taste of him, the way he's losing his mind for me. All for me.

When it seems like he's about to come, he eases off and loosens his hold. I'm about to take him deeper, pull him into it before he can stop me, but he grabs my chin hard and yanks me up. "Not until I say. You don't decide when I come, or even when you come. Not until I say you can."

I swallow and nod, my mouth aching from the abuse.

"Now, I'll give you a little reward. Stand up and put that pretty cunt right in my face."

My mouth flops open, and I'm about to protest. Still, he slaps my ass hard enough to make it sting, so I hop to my feet, and he doesn't even let me get my balance before his hand is around my thigh and his tongue is swiping across my clit.

"Fucking hell," I stammer and catch my hands on the wall above him.

He hums against my skin, sending a shock wave of sensation through me. "Spread your legs wider. I want to fuck you with my tongue."

I brace my hands and spread my feet. One hits the side of the bathtub, but the other can get a bit farther, giving him enough room to do what he wants.

He uses his free head, cutting through my wet flesh with his fingers and slipping two fingers deep. "So fucking wet. You taste like heaven," he whispers against my skin, and I squeeze my eyes closed, already fighting the urge to soak him with my cum.

"Don't stop."

After a second, he switches his fingers, adding a third, and gives my clit a little bite, and I swear my soul almost pops free of my skin. Good gods, where did he learn to do this?

He laps at me like an ice cream cone until my knees shake while he fucks me with his fingers.

I'm so close. So fucking close. Just a little bit more. I'm rocking my hips into his face, seeking the sensation when he stops. He pulls his hand away and leans his head back onto the wall. "Get down here and ride me."

So far, he hasn't done a single thing I haven't eagerly signed on for. My body is humming with the need for release. I crouch over him and move to sit on his length, but he pats my hips and swirls his fingers. "No, turn around."

I don't argue. I shift my weight and move to sit on him the opposite way and ride him backward. The second I ease the still-wet tip of him into my entrance, I moan.

His fingers clutch where my hip meets my thigh, and he lifts me higher, rising up with me until I'm on my hands and knees in front of him.

Well, okay then.

"I'm going to use you hard, Malyshka. I hope you can take as much as you think you can."

I don't have time to answer before he slams his full length inside me. But he doesn't let me get far, using his free hand to hold my shoulder, pulling me back into him while he brutally pounds at me from behind.

He stretches me more than I'm used to, and everything screams in pain as my body adjusts. Then like a light switch, the pain is gone, and wave after wave of brutal pleasure chases it.

He curls his hand from my shoulder to my neck and lifts my back against his chest so I stay impaled on him but upright.

"Yes, that's it," he says against my hair. Now I can look at those pretty round tits bounce while I fuck you.

I can only whimper while he uses me. His body fills me completely. Each pass of his dick inside me is a lightning strike of pure sensation. After a few minutes, I hear a whimper, and it takes me a minute to figure out it's coming from me.

I clutch at his forearm, and he squeezes my neck tighter, cutting my airway by the tiniest bit. For some reason, it makes everything brighter, the room, the edge of pain at my core, the wave after wave of pleasure.

"Please," I whisper, barely making a sound with his tight grasp around my neck.

He slides his mouth up to my cheek. "Please, what? Tell me what you want."

The whimper I make is embarrassing, but I can't do anything else. "I need more."

"Use your words. Tell me what you need."

I hold his wrist tighter, surging back into him as he pushes forward into me. "I need my clit touched. Please."

"Then touch it. But if you come before I say you can, I'll fuck your face instead and deny you any further release." His teeth graze my jaw, and then my neck as he moves faster, surging harder until all I feel is his breathless pace and my own aching body answering.

I reach down and rub my clit, needing the stimulation to push me toward my orgasm, but I'm careful. If he doesn't let me come, I might go insane.

He shoves my head forward again, and I fall, using my hands to catch myself, losing the rhythm I'd generated at my clit. "Flick your clit, Malyshka. We are going to come together. Be ready when I am."

I pick up the pace, grinding my fingers against me, my nails scraping skin that will be raw in a couple of hours.

He brings his hand down to my hip and uses it to pull me back onto him. "When I can use both hands, I'm going to fuck this tight little asshole too."

The idea in my imagination is enough to send me headlong toward my orgasm. I have to slow my hand for fear of reaching it before he orders it.

"Ready?" he growls, his voice low and jagged. He's still stretching me tight, and his thighs slap against mine with every brutal thrust.

I whimper and then realize he's waiting for an answer. "Yes. Please. Let me come."

"Mmm...I like when you beg. It makes me even fucking harder." He moves faster, which seems impossible, and I rub my clit harder, trying to match him thrust for thrust.

"Now!" He bellows, dragging my battered body back into him hard enough that my hip will be bruised. For some reason, his order, and the permission that comes with it, shoves me over the cliff of my orgasm. I go into a free fall, stars dancing in my vision as he pumps into me harder and harder.

I'm about to ask if he's going to pull out, but I'm breathless and can barely form the words when he lets out a low moan rolling into a grunt, and I feel the hot wet jet of his cum inside me.

It should terrify me, but some primal part of me wants his cum. Wants him inside me until we both are completely sated.

He relaxes, his body rigid with tension, easing until he pats my hip and pulls out. The wet heat slides down my inner thighs, and I can barely move, my knees aching, my palms aching, and even my head pounding from what feels like a change in altitude.

He gently helps me sit back and then turns me on the cold tile so I can straddle his lap again. "Are you all right?"

I nod and lay my forehead against his shoulder. "Just let me sit for a second, and I'll leave you alone."

He pulls my hair out from between us and wraps it around his hand, not in a fist, more in wonder. But I don't see what he does next because my eyes are already drifting closed, my body sated for what feels like the very first time.

18

IVAN

This time, waking from a doze with a warm woman on my lap, even with my hand cuffed, I figure out my surroundings quickly. The dungeon is gone, and right now, all there is is her. I breathe in the scent of her hair. It's clean from the shower she must have taken in the other bathroom. But underneath is something that is all her. I fill my lungs with it, let it soothe and calm the raw edges in my chest. For the first time in a while, there's no anger, no pain, nothing but her and me.

I flex my numb fingers in the cuff and give myself a survey. The drugs seem to have worn off, or finally getting off has dulled the effects. Either way, I'm grateful. I don't linger on the thoughts for fear the rage will charge back full force, and I'll march off to burn that place to the ground without a plan.

I gently shift her in my lap, our bodies sticky where we meet. When she flexes around me, I start to grow stiff again. I wasn't gentle with her, so I want to make sure she's not in pain before I sink into her depths again, and I will be doing it again.

It takes some maneuvering with her weight on my lap to reach where I stashed the handcuff key. Once I free my hand, I take a second to massage the feeling back into my hand and forearm. She mumbles and snuggles against my chest. How can this woman have such softness in her after everything she's been through?

I swipe her hair off her face to look at her. Soft cheeks, long lashes, and lips meant to wrap around a man's dick. Once my hand stops tingling, I easily stand with her in my arms and step into the shower.

She protests as I ease her to her feet. "Why can't we just go back to bed?"

I turn on the water, then face her under the spray once it warms. This tub isn't big enough for both of us, so I take charge of tipping her head under the spray to wash her hair. "We have things to do. People to kill. Stuff to explode."

Her eyes pop open, but I shake my head, and she squeezes them tight again, so she doesn't get soap in them. "Explode?"

I finish rinsing her and steer her under the spray more fully before grabbing the soap and lathering up her full breasts. Her nipples pucker under my palms, but I don't have time to play with her. Not when my team is likely going out of their minds wondering what happened.

And I find I want to give them an update. If only to meet all of their eyes and ensure they are safe. They are the closest thing I have to a family in this world.

I wash her thoroughly but quickly and then swipe the soap over myself, which goes faster. When I turn the water off, she's already leaning out to grab a couple of fluffy white towels from a nearby rack.

"Get some clothes on. I'll call Kai and have him bring something you can wear that might fit better."

Her eyes widen. "Kai?"

"You've met him at the casino before, no doubt, or at least seen him around."

Something chases through her eyes before she clears it away and nods. "Yes. I've seen him. Why do you need to call him?"

I tilt her chin up and try not to feel something by the way she leans into me at the small touch. Her terry cloth covered chest against my bare one. "Because Kai can get me intel and supplies. Both of which we need right now. I'm not going after your father with no information and getting myself captured again. I'm going to take him down completely. I can't wait to feel that bastard's neck in my hands as I watch the life drain from his eyes."

Now she really does look scared, but curiously, not of me. For me? I thumb the side of her cheek, reveling in how soft and smooth her skin is. "Don't worry about me, Malyshka. I can take care of myself. Or are you scared for him and what I'm going to do when I finally get my hands on him?"

She shakes her head. "No. I don't care much for what happens to him as long as I don't have to go near him."

I don't tell her I expect her to be with me when I kill him. Instead, I turn her toward the bedroom. "Go put some clothes on. I'll make my call, and then we can eat something." My stomach is now roiling uncomfortably from lack of food. I fear I'll be useless to keep her safe until I eat something.

She goes into the closet to slip into some clean clothes. All of them are for men, but I note that we should add some female clothing just in case the newly paired-up teammates need clothes. Andrea always said if she needs a safe house, she doesn't give a shit what she's wearing.

I grab clean clothes out of the dresser. Nothing fancy. A dress shirt and a pair of pants. Enough to cover me, not enough to intimidate anyone. While she dresses, I head into the kitchen and throw a couple of sandwiches together. Peanut butter on warm bread is enough to sate the ache in my stomach. I grab the second burner phone, the one I keep in case of emergencies or the off chance I break a phone or lose one, and hit the pre-programmed number on it.

Kai answers after two rings. "Are you still alive?"

"Fucker," I say, not bothering to stifle the affection in my tone. "For now, at least. I need some supplies, and I need information on these assholes. I'm ripping that place apart."

"We're ready and will help."

I shake my head and then speak because he can't see me. "No. I'm doing this on my own. You guys stay there, and if I need to call you in, I will."

There's a long silence, and I wait for whatever bullshit Kai is trying to come up with to convince me against my plan.

After another agonizing few seconds, he says, "Okay. I'll send Michail with supplies and keys to your personal safe house."

I hate that he knows what it means to be held captive as intimately as I do. But it's the only reason he's letting me go on my own right now. I don't bother to thank you because we both have the knowledge. "I'll keep you posted and let you know if I need anything."

"Stay safe, my friend, and give them hell."

I hang up and squeeze the phone tightly. The memories of the last week surge up enough that my sandwich threatens to make a return visit. When Cilla exits the bedroom, she rushes to my side, eyeing me where I have my hands braced against the counter, breathing against the gut-roiling emotion threatening to drag me under.

Her hands cup my cheeks, and she ducks under my arms to put her face close to mine, but I don't let her pull me closer. Not when I'm in this mood.

"Hey," she whispers. "You're here. You're safe."

The sound of her voice twines through me, easing the edges of my shame, my fear, my anger, all of it. When I can breathe again, I meet her eyes. "Sit. We need to talk about your father's operation."

Her voice is barely a whisper. "But I don't know anything."

I put a sandwich in her hand, steer her to the dining room table, and plop her on a wooden chair. "Sit, eat, and I'll ask the questions. You probably know more than you think you do."

She takes a bite of the sandwich, her eyes locked on me. I rove my gaze down her body to the plain T-shirt and baggy jeans she's rolled up at the ankle.

Shrugging, she speaks between chews. "They're too big, but there wasn't anything else besides suits."

I take the chair beside hers and slide it close enough that I can touch her knees. "Kai. Even if his life is in danger, he will look damn good."

As if she doesn't know what to say to that, she takes another big bite and chews slowly while she searches my face for something. What, I'm not sure of yet.

"Does the rest of your extended family know about your father's operation or how lucrative it might be for him?"

Her forehead furrows almost as if she's thinking deeply. "I don't know. He doesn't tell me that kind of stuff or anything, really. It's not like we have long chats about business over the dinner table at night. I barely see him unless he drugged me or orders me to do something disgusting."

"Something disgusting?"

She gulps and drops her eyes. "Like whoring myself to get to you."

Ah. She's scared of reminding me, like I plan to get revenge the second she mentions it. I grab her chin and tilt her face up to look into her eyes again.

"Fine. Besides your father, who is in charge over there?"

This time she thinks, her eyes taking on a far-off look and then focusing on me again. "Probably the doctor. One of the doctors he employs who helps him with his tinkering, or whatever he calls it. Chemists who help him make his drugs. He's trained himself, but he likes to experiment and likes others around so he can discuss his experiments with them. He has a big ego."

She doesn't need to remind me of that. Arthur's ego is bigger than his compound. "Yeah, I got that at our first meeting. That, and he's a huge fucking douche."

This makes her chuckle, and the sound of her laughter loosens something in my chest enough that I feel like I can breathe deeper. It's nothing but a connection born from our shared experience, but I don't question when something helps me stay in control of my emotions. She's helped me do that from day one.

"What else can you tell me? Anything about a weak spot in his compound? Anywhere in the building you used to sneak out as a teenager?"

She takes another bite of her sandwich and shakes her head. "No," she mumbles. "I didn't exactly have a normal childhood or normal teenage years. Not when my family is filled with fucking assholes and pedophiles."

Fair point. "Anything else you can tell me at all that might help?"

Her lashes are damp when she meets my eyes again. Concern swirls deep within.

"What happens to me now?"

I meet her gaze head-on. "What do you think happens to you now? What do you want, Priscilla?"

I watch her face closely. Not for her to lie but to see if I can spot it, to see what she wants. I don't know if it's for herself or me, but she gives me nothing and says nothing that clues me in on what she wants or needs.

Gently, I tug her free hand into mine, the scent of peanut

butter between us. "For now, you belong to me. No one will touch you. No one will hurt you. No one will get near you without my say-so. Do you understand?"

She nods and sets what's left of her sandwich on the table, and places her hand on top of mine. "Then what?"

"Then we will kill every motherfucker in that building, starting at the top and working our way down to the bottom. Not one person involved in this drug operation will be left standing when I'm through with that hellhole."

19

CILLA

As much as I enjoy the idea of punishing everyone who hurt me, killing everyone is not what I want. I've seen so much death and violence in my life that the idea of causing more turns my stomach.

I pull away from him and stand to pace. "Can't we just revel in being free instead of needing to cause more death?"

Sometimes, I fantasize about murdering them all, even going so far as to promise myself in my head. But if someone wrapped my palm around a gun, I'm not entirely sure I'd be able to pull that trigger.

"Freedom doesn't mean what you think it does in this world. You're never really free. You're just running on borrowed time, waiting for the moment when your enemy gets the upper hand. It's a game of wits, of being a little smarter than the person in front of you."

His response doesn't make me feel better, and I swallow hard. "Ummm...I'm not sure what I can do in this situation. I'm not smart, or—"

He stomps over, takes hold of my chin hard, and forces me to look at him. "Don't speak about yourself like that. As to what you do, well..." He smiles, but it's more unhinged than gleeful. "The season is open. I can blow every one of these motherfuckers to bits, and no one can stop me."

I stay still and calm in his grasp. After a few more seconds, he releases me and walks toward the window in the living room to stare out.

His voice is too quiet when he asks, "Why don't you want these assholes dead?"

I wrap my arms around my middle. "I never said I didn't want them dead. I just don't think I can be the one to kill them."

His back is stiff, and I don't like that I can't see his face. To try to read what he's thinking. Not that he's easy to read at all. The only time I can sense his emotions is when he's angry. To be fair, it's what I have the most experience with so far.

I take a few steps toward him.

He stands like a sentinel, straight-backed, blocking a good portion of the window. Some slivers of light break around the outline of him. "I just don't understand how you can let them get away with brutalizing you for years and just walk away. Forgiveness might be in your nature, but it sure as hell isn't in mine."

I swallow hard, staring at his back, willing him to turn and look at me. "There's a difference between forgiveness and self-preservation. All I want is to be free of them all. That's all I've ever wanted. To be free of my family name to live my own life."

The tension grows tight, pulling between us despite what we shared earlier in the bathroom. Maybe because of it. Both of us think we're someone we aren't. Someone each of us needed in a painful moment.

I hug myself tight again, needing comfort, even if I won't get it from him. "No, everyone can live their lives surrounded by pain and death. I've paid my dues; now I want out."

"I don't live this life this way because I have a choice. You may remember you, and your father kidnapped me, so what comes next is all on you."

It's been a while since the rage in his eyes made me scared. At least for myself. When he turns his cold eyes to mine, I feel a hot flash of anger in my belly. I've more than made up for my mistakes, but with a heart full of vengeance, he's not going to let me forget my role in his capture. How long until I'm the only person left he needs to get revenge on?

I step back, keeping my eyes on his face. "Good to know how you feel. Thank you. That will make leaving a lot easier."

He doesn't let me retreat. "You thought what? We'd get free, set up house, and start a little nuclear family?"

It's stupid to rile him, but I roll my eyes anyway. "I'm not an idiot." Instead of getting into the details, I sigh. "Forget it. As I said, I want to be free of all this. Spend the rest of my life safe and bored."

He bears down on me again, snatching my bicep in his iron hold. "You can leave when I say you can leave. In other words, you can leave when I'm done with you."

I swallow hard, unsure of what to say to that. It doesn't matter since he doesn't give me room to speak, placing his other hand around my neck. He doesn't squeeze but simply holds me in place, not allowing me to move another inch away from him.

I hold my breath when he leans down, his mouth millimeters from mine. "Open the door."

My heart is pounding as I figure out his words. He flexes his fingers on my throat for a moment, then gently shoves me toward the door. I don't even consider if I should or what it might mean for me. I open it.

On the other side stands a tall man, glossy black ringlets brushing his cheeks. I blink for a second to check if he's real.

"Open the door for Michail, *Malyshka*," Ivan orders again.

I hold it open farther and stare as the man enters, barely sparing me a glance as he eyes Ivan.

The man claps him on the shoulder and then drops a bag at his feet. "You scared the shit out of me, you bastard."

They hug, Ivan wrapping his hand around the back of the other man's neck, squeezing tight. I'm still staring between them when they separate, though neither spares me even a look. That's fine. I'm not a woman who needs attention. I'm greedy for information about Ivan, watching them carefully, hoping one of them gives me something.

They whisper a moment, and Michail slides something small across Ivan's palm. A key, maybe?

When they finish, Michail faces me, his eyes dark and almost feral as he sweeps me a glance from my head to my toes. "You were at the casino."

I gulp and nod.

"You hurt him again, and I'll kill you myself." With that little tidbit, he leaves, closing the door behind him.

Ivan crosses to me, the bag in hand. "Let's go."

Wait. What? He takes my hand and turns me to the door. "Where are we going?"

We step outside, and I notice a slight chill in the mid-afternoon air. "Somewhere better and more secure than this place. I need to plan and a better place to do said planning."

There's a car waiting for us. Shiny. Black. Nondescript but definitely high-end. He crosses to the driver's side, tosses the bag in the back, and I scramble to the passenger seat to the right side of the car and buckle up.

Our flight the other day feels a million years ago. Ivan is tense and silent as we pull out of the driveway. The towers of the city loom closer as we drive. I don't know how long we drive for, fifteen, twenty minutes maybe, can't be more than that, but again, I'm not keeping track of time. The car rolls to a stop, and we park outside a shiny high-rise.

This is not the casino or the building I know his team lives in. Something bad starts to fester in my gut, and I know this won't end well.

Ivan grabs the bag and tosses the keys to a small, suited man, who races out of the building. When I don't get out of the car immediately, he comes around and opens the door, his knuckles white on top of the window. "Get the fuck out of the car, Cilla. I won't fight with you right now. I'll merely pull you out and toss you over my shoulder, and later we'll discuss your punishment."

No matter what he thinks, I don't have a fight in me either way. He leads me to an elevator, then up several floors, and stops outside a textured chrome door. We go inside, and I stop in the entryway. My gaze swings around the room as I drink it in.

The place is huge, wide open, with windows lining one whole side of the room. The furniture is minimal and low, so it doesn't block the view.

"What is this place? Another safe house?"

He sighs. "Sort of. I have my place at the casino. This one Adrian bought me to use, but I rarely come here. Most of the time, I forget it exists. So I guess it's my apartment?"

I stare around, looking for something that speaks about him. Anything? There's a low stack of glasses on a bar around the corner and a small table but not much else. Even the massive pieces of art on the walls don't really feel like him. He's got a brutal sort of beauty that I don't see in any part of this cool, calm space.

After inspecting the place, I tiptoe into the room he disappeared into. It's a bedroom, the furniture the same as the other room, minimal and functional. One big bed is pushed out of the formation of the room so it sits flush against the wall of windows. Like you could roll over and fall right out if the glass wasn't there. "Is this your room?" I don't even give him a chance to speak. "And if so, where am I sleeping?"

He hangs up a couple of things in the closet and flips off the light. "You will sleep here with me. I don't want you out of my sight."

His words make me jolt. "What? What could I possibly do?"

His eyes narrow, and he skirts around me to face the windows. "I don't know. That's the point. Until I understand you better and your motivations, I don't want you far from my sights or reach."

I stare at the ceiling to hold the tears threatening to slip free at bay. When I know I won't cry in front of him anymore, I meet his eyes and nod.

"Fine. Do what you want with me. Everyone else does."

His jaw tightens, and he turns, stalking back over to me and stopping so we are chest to chest. "Don't you dare imply I'm anything like *them*."

I let him see what I think in my eyes. Let the accusation hang between us. It might fester and make things worse, but I don't care. He thinks he is so much better than them. That he can take what he wants from me, when he wants, and because he makes it pleasurable, protects me, that I'll say thank you and curl up at his feet.

I glare, and he glares back, his mouth so close to mine I can feel his warm breath on my lips and chin. Another minute passes, if my pounding heart is any indication, and he breaks away, stalking back into the living room.

He grabs something by the door and heads into the other space opposite this room. I follow because what the fuck else am I going to do right now?

I enter to watch him place some weapons on a very intricate wall. The entire room is a peg board that holds various guns, knives, and other sharp objects. They gleam under the overhead lighting. I should be afraid, but strangely, I'm not. If anything, I'm curious and intrigued.

Drawers line the floor, which I assume contains ammunition for all of these lovely weapons. "Holy shit. You have your own damn armory."

He places a few things on the display. "There's a bigger one in the penthouse. This is just my own collection."

Forget only being curious… I'm pretty sure I'm almost turned on. My insides heat, my core clenching around nothing.

"So what now? You're going to babysit me until you slaughter what's left of my family?"

He doesn't look at me as he speaks. "You want to watch? Or would you rather I lock you up the entire time? If I had my way, you'd have a gun in your hand and be by my side helping me. I think one day, you'll regret not taking things into your own hands. You'll regret not getting your own revenge."

I shake my head and slump against the drawers, sitting on top of one set. "No. I'm not like you. I don't need blood on my hands to satisfy some warped part of me. I know what I am and what I've done, and when the time comes for me to die, I won't regret anything. Revenge isn't what I'm out for. I want to be free."

20

IVAN

Twice in the night, Cilla tried to sneak out from under my arm. She's had practice at being silent, but I've had more practice at waking under threat. The second she twitched, I dragged her back down beside me. The scent of soap and her body mingling with mine soothed me right back to sleep.

She's not leaving my side until I take out her bastard of a father and his whole damn family, and if she tries to run, I'll hunt her down alongside him. It might hurt a little to lose her at this point, but I'm sure I'll adjust. I've had to adjust to losing people over the years, so this wouldn't be anything new.

I roll over as the sun rises and stare out across the chrome maze through the window. Since I'm usually at the casino, I don't come here. Hell, I forget the place exists most of the time, but moments like this...I should try to remember. Moments when my mind doesn't feel ready to explode with the weight of my anger.

Cilla shifts in the bed beside me and then jerks my arm off her waist. "Are you awake now? May I finally get up and go to the bathroom?"

I scratch at my head and stare her down. "Don't fucking pretend I kept you from pissing. You wanted out of bed so you could sneak out of the apartment. Don't worry, tomorrow night, you can get up to your heart's content. There's an alarm on the door. If you so much as breathe near the door handle, it'll let me know."

Her scowl makes me smile as she heads into the bathroom and slams the door.

I head into the closet and grab a few items Michail brought. A white silk strappy shirt with a delicate fringe of lace, a matching pair of white lace underwear, black skinny jeans that will mean I can stare at the round curve of her ass anytime I want, and a pair of black leather boots to complete the look.

I lay the clothing on the bed and smooth the fringe flat. It's pretty and fragile, just like she is. It'll be important to remember that fact as we continue the plan.

When she exits the bathroom, I'm already dressed in a white button-down, slacks, and shoes buffed to a high shine. She narrows her eyes as I snap on my watch.

I nod to the pile of clothing. "That's for you. Get dressed. We have somewhere to be this morning."

I'm almost positive she'll argue, but she chooses to surprise me and presses her lips together. A moment later, she drops her gaze, lifts the hem of her borrowed T-shirt, and tosses it to the floor.

I swallow as I'm gifted with the gorgeous sight of her naked skin. Her nipples are already stiff and teasing my control. One glimpse, and I'm done for.

"If you wanted to stay in so I could fuck you into a puddle, all you had to do was ask."

She lets out a little squeak as she shimmies into the underwear, then clears her throat. "No. I just figured you'd already seen it all. What's the point in modesty now."

I step closer and stare down while she continues dressing, this time faster. As if the little scraps of lace will keep me from taking what I want. "You're lucky we have an appointment, or I'd show you exactly how little I care about modesty. You'd be naked every day, so I can slide my fingers between your thighs anytime I want."

She stares at me, eyes wide, fingers stalling on the edge of her shirt. "You, what?"

I lean down, bite the tiny dip in her chin, and then turn her toward the door. "Let's go. We can talk about it more when we get back."

She doesn't pull away when I capture her hand and hold it until we reach my car in the underground garage. Usually, the valet brings it around, but I'm in a hurry, and we are already running late.

El Corredora lives on the same side of town, so it's not far to find my top drug contact in the city. His security buzzes us in when we step up to the camera. The top floor of the building is a twenty-four seven party. Any kind of entertainment you could want, El Corredora—the runner—can provide. He's not a member of society, having his own organization to answer to, but he does work with many of its prominent members.

We enter the room, and she stops. I have to wrap my arm around her waist and tug her forward. "Come on, Malyshka. He doesn't bite. Besides, it'll take a minute to find him in this crowd." I lean down so she can hear me above the bumping bass of the music.

Everywhere we look, people are doing drugs, fucking, or dancing. A few less-adventurous souls are chatting on low couches strewn around the room.

I spot Eric across the room and weave through the people to get to him. He rises when we reach the low cream-colored couch he's lounging on. "Ivan. Man. It's been a while since I've seen you here. Do you need something? Or I guess the better question is, are you here for business or pleasure?"

His gaze shifts to Cilla at my side, and he sweeps her an appreciative glance that makes me tighten my hold on her. "Business, I'm afraid. I need to know if you've recently seen an influx of designer drugs."

He blinks and shakes his head. "You know I don't traffic with small businessmen."

"It's not that. I'm not here on Adrian's behalf. I want to know if you've seen anything hitting the city markets with strange additives. Promises that the drugs can't keep?"

His lips thin as he narrows his eyes. He shoves out of his chair and crosses the room, beckoning us to follow. We move to the corner of the room. In as much privacy as this place affords, he leans in, forcing me to stare down at him. It's not a position many men are comfortable with.

"Look. There have been a few instances lately. One drug that promises the best sex of your life if taken by both partners. Another that supposedly turns people into zombies, walking and talking mind control."

I risk a glance at Cilla and find her gaze wide.

"Eric, call me if you get any info on either of these or who might be moving them, selling them, any of that shit. Even though I'm not here for Adrian, I know he'd consider it a special favor if you help us."

He nods, eyes glimmering at the idea of Adrian owing him something. Having Adrian on your side in this town is something you more than want. I lead Cilla back out, relieved we didn't have to stay too long, mixed with the crowd and noise.

On the ride down, I study her. "Did you see anyone you recognize?"

She shakes her head and wraps her arms around her body, almost like she's hugging herself. *Shit.* I forgot to get her a jacket when I asked Michail to pick out some clothing. I'll remedy that soon enough.

"No, no one I recognize."

"Then why did you look so scared when we were talking to Eric?"

She stares at her feet and taps her toe on the expensive tile. "Because I recognize the drugs he spoke about. The sex one you've already tried for yourself. The other one, my father has been developing for a long time. It's more of a mind-control drug. I didn't think...or well...I don't know if it actually works or not. Sometimes, he'd test drugs on me, and I don't remember, so...he could have tested that one on me too." Her voice breaks at the end, and I wrap my hands around her shoulders and pull her to my chest. The mere reminder of how pathetic and shitty her father is makes me want to kill him and bring him back to life so I can do it all over again. There's a protectiveness that this woman brings out in me for her, and I don't understand why.

"He won't touch you again. He won't make you take anything you don't want. I can promise you that."

She sniffs, snuggling tighter against me. "You can't promise me that. If he gets ahold of me again, he'll punish me for running and embarrassing him. Knowing him, he will probably kill me."

I stiffen and squeeze her closer. "He'll have to get through me first."

"Why do you even care? I'm no one to you. Less than no one, actually." She lifts her face to look up at me. "I'm probably on your own personal revenge list right now."

A tear streaks down her soft cheek, and I catch it with my thumb and bring it to my lips. The salty tang explodes against my tongue. "What I care about isn't something you need to worry about. Now, let's go back to the apartment and determine if these drugs have been seen elsewhere in the city."

When we return to the apartment, though, Adrian is sitting in a chair facing out the window, his arms on the edges, his hands form in steeples in the middle under his chin. As usual, he's in a suit, looking like a walking couture ad or some shit. Just like Kai usually does.

"Adrian," I say by way of greeting.

His eyes snag on Cilla, staying as she slips off her boots and leaves them by the door. Her warm feet make ghost footprints on the hardwood leading to the couch.

Adrian doesn't bother with pleasantries. I'm sure he knows the entire situation already. More than I do, even. "We have a problem."

I sit on the couch and pat the space beside me until she sits, keeping her distance. Fuck that shit. I pull her into me, needing her scent to chase away my demons because I know I'm not about to like what Adrian is going to say.

"Just spit it out."

Adrian, face impassive, flicks his gaze to Cilla. "Your father sent a formal request to the council, asking them to intercede on your behalf. He maintains you cannot care for yourself, that you need special care, and that Ivan has kidnapped you for his own..." He grimaces. "...twisted ends."

I try to breathe through the tidal wave welling inside me, but it's too much. It's crushing me from the inside out. "What the fuck is that asshole playing at?"

I shift forward to stand, needing to move, to walk, to fucking break something, but Cilla grabs my arm and tugs me closer. She looks at Adrian again. "What does he want? What were his demands?"

Adrian shifts forward in the chair and braces his elbows on his knees. His knuckles are bruised, and he looks tired. Something I hadn't noticed, so wrapped up in what was happening in my world.

"He demands the council return you to him immediately, and if you are harmed in any way, the Doubeck family pays restitution for any injury."

"Restitution," she repeats slowly like she doesn't understand the word. "I'm not sure what he really wants or even what game he's playing. He likes to think he's five moves ahead, so he does have some kind of plan here."

Adrian's lips twist into a hardened smile. "Lucky for him, I'm good at playing games. I'm also good with a gun when I get tired of them."

Cilla blinks and leans closer to me. "So what do we do?"

Adrian shoves out of the chair and meets my gaze head-on. It takes a minute for things to clink. Fuck. Fucking Fuck. Fuck. Fuck.

Cilla stares between us, obviously able to read me better than she can read Adrian. Fair. Not many people can read him.

He walks out without another word, and I jerk out of Cilla's grasp to pace the floor.

She hugs her waist. "What did I miss? What's going on?"

I can't think this way. Not when my mind rages, and all I want is the hot wet feel of blood across my knuckles. I kneel on the floor before her, grab her face, and pull her in for a kiss. She doesn't resist, falling against my chest as I cradle her face and sweep my tongue into her mouth. In seconds, with just this tiny taste of her, I feel calmer. Even as my body wakes, my cock hardens, and I can only think about touching her now.

I'll take the temptation of her skin over the inferno of my rage any day.

21

CILLA

It would be so easy to lose myself in the heat of his mouth or the feel of his calloused hands on my bare skin. Except I worry that his kissing me is an act of desperation or a distraction, and I'm tired of living in the dark about what I'm doing or being involved in.

I gently pull my face from his, even as blood pumps under my skin, my body wanting more of what he's offering. "Stop. Wait. What's happening here? What's wrong?"

He's got that manic look in his eyes again. The one who says he's on the wrong side of control needs to take the edge off. My body tightens, remembering what he feels like when he's out of control. "It's nothing you need to worry about right now."

That's the absolute worst thing he could have said. "Don't speak to me like I'm a child, especially when I think whatever is going on has everything to do with me, nor do I appreciate you hiding things from me."

When he narrows his eyes at my sharp tone, I know I've gone one step too far.

He eases his big hand around my neck, holding me in place while he stands. "You want to know what's going on? *Fine.*" His voice turns to granite. "Your father has thrown down the gauntlet. Demanding we send you back to him or..."

"Or? Or..." I whisper. "Or what?" Panic builds low in my belly. "I'm not going back to him, Ivan. I'm not."

He flexes his fingers, applying the tiniest hint of pressure, and it's enough to send a wave of tingles and heat through me. "Why the fuck do you think I'm so pissed off. He expects me to send you back to him. He wants me to send you back. It's a punishment for you and for me since he knows I'm trying to keep you safe from him."

"So then, what do we do? How do we keep ourselves safe and ensure he doesn't involve the council further. When I was working there, I heard rumors in the casino that the Doubeck family is trying to be on its best behavior since many were speculating you guys were involved with that FBI agent that got arrested."

His jaw tightens, his nostrils flaring. "Oh yeah? What else did you hear?"

I shake my head frantically. "Nothing. Only that the two guys were saying Adrian and his family are trying to stay on the right side of the council for now. To calm everything down for the moment."

He scans my face, his gaze landing on the swell of my cleavage. "When Valentina and Adrian got together, her father tried to pull something similar."

I suck in a breath, knowing she's safe and sound right now at Adrian's side. "And what did they do to make him reconsider?"

His eyes snap to mine. "They got married. Marriage supersedes the request of the father since the council has no rules on who gets married and when, or even how."

I shake my head. That doesn't seem right. "Wait a minute. You're not suggesting what I think you're suggesting?" I try to wiggle out of his hold, but it only makes him grip me tighter and pull me closer to his body. Heat radiates all around me as he towers above me. "No. We can't. I'll run before I let that happen." My thoughts swim like I'm in a fishbowl with nowhere to escape. "Let me go, and I'll run, and the council can come in here and search to their heart's content. We both know they won't find me."

"That's what your father wants. He wants me to turn you over or for you to run. Either way, he'll get you and punish you for making him work harder to get what he wants. I hate to break it to you, Cilla, but things are no longer about just whether you live or die. Multiple lives are hanging in the balance now."

I clutch his shirt, trying to pull him closer so I can feel him better while also pushing him away. "I don't know what that means. Just let me go. He won't find me. I've got a plan I've worked on for years. If I want to disappear, I'll be able to disappear."

He trails his free hand from the back of my neck down the curve of my spine, and splays his fingers over my ass. "You won't be able to hide well enough. I'm sorry, but there's nothing left now but to make the right choice."

My breathing comes out in pants as I let my eyes fall closed to surrender to the sensation of his hand kneading my ass, pressing me harder into his erection, which is growing against my stomach. "I don't understand. What's the right choice?"

When he releases his grasp, I draw in a full breath, even though he wasn't really preventing me from breathing. I'm powerless against the sensation of his full lips sliding from my earlobe to my collarbone and back up. "The season is open right now. Do you know what that means?"

I swallow and nod once. "Yes. I know what it means."

He lifts his face up to stare into my eyes. "No. I don't think you do. With the season open, nothing is stopping me from walking into your father's house, shooting every person in the head, and walking back out. Then doing the same to the council. Right now, everything is fair game. It will close again in a few weeks, so we don't have much time."

"So you're saying," I whisper, my voice shaking with the effort to stay calm. "My choice is to marry you, or you're going to kill a whole bunch of people?"

He shrugs.

Shrugs.

Who the fuck is this guy?

I try to pull away, but his grip is an iron shackle wrapped around me. "No. You don't get away from me that easily. I've never hidden who I am. You, yourself, called me an animal when we met. Just because this animal has a taste for your flesh doesn't mean it's any different. Besides, I'll only kill those who want to take you from me. Anyone else is free to carry on unless they were involved in my kidnapping. Those assholes are dead regardless."

"I can't let you kill everyone. That's not...you can't. It would be my fault. I can't let that happen."

He steps away and turns me toward the door. "Then I guess we will get married."

"When?" My voice doesn't shake this time, but I can't bask in its pride as he leads me out to the elevator. Hell, I don't even have my shoes on. He's carrying the boots he gave me in his hands. "Where are we going? What's happening?"

"We're getting married now."

I try to tug him to a stop, but he's immovable, still dragging me along to the car. "Wait. No. We can't just get married right now."

He doesn't look at me as he speaks. "You think your father will wait? That he'll sit on his heels and let the council take their time? No. He's already mobilizing who he needs to in order to get them to pound down our door and take you away. The faster we get this done, the safer you'll be."

We climb into the car, and I'm still considering jumping out the door to get away. How did this happen? I can't even reconcile it in my mind when we've pulled up outside a high-rise, and I'm led up to what I assume is the heart of the Doubeck domain.

The foyer has white rose petals and a small woman I've only seen once standing next to Adrian. Her belly rounded, stretching the fabric of her pink sweater. She steps forward when we enter. "You must be Priscilla, right?"

Ivan nudges me out of the elevator toward her. "Uh, yes, you can call me Cilla, though. If you want to."

She smiles, white and bright, making me feel even worse. "You can call me Val. Come on, let's get you ready."

I follow her to a bedroom, and she lays out a white dress on the bed. It's long and elegant and everything I'm not. "Michail told us your size so we could grab something for you to wear."

"It's white."

Her eyes drop to the dress. "Yes?"

"They told you I'm a whore, right? I can't wear white on my wedding day." It's an excuse, but right now, I'm clinging to anything that can get me out of this. Get Ivan out of this. He's already helped me enough, and now he's being punished for it.

Val steps forward, taking my hands, enveloping me in a soft scent I can't pinpoint. "We kind of specialize in marriage under strange circumstances around here. Ivan is only trying to help."

"What if I get him killed? What if helping me is why someone uses me to kill him or do worse, like before?" Even though it's only been a short time, I can already feel something in my chest telling me I have to protect him and keep him safe, no matter what.

Val chuckles. "Ivan is strong, and he knows what he wants. If he didn't want to do this, you'd be on the next plane to South America. Trust him to protect you, and he will."

I'm out of excuses and the will to fight. She helps me into the dress, her baby bump nudging me every time she moves within a foot of me.

When I'm dressed, she gently braids my hair and gives me a wide smile. "Let's get this done so you'll be safe." She rubs her hand over her belly absentmindedly.

I follow her back out to the foyer to find Ivan standing in front of a priest wearing a tuxedo. Good lord, if that man wasn't made to wear them. He shaved, so his face is clean, and I can see his tattoos trailing across his knuckles and up his neck. Seeing each one makes me want to trace the patterns with my tongue.

I step forward, and he takes my hands. "Keep looking at me like that, Malyshka, and we're not going to make it through this thing."

It seems like I blink, and it's over. He slides a heavy diamond onto my finger, and then he's pulling my face to his for a kiss. By his standards, it's chaste.

We get about five seconds to look at each other. My insides are scrambled, and I'm not sure if this is real or maybe a hallucination my brain has cooked up because I'm trying to cope with whatever fucked-up experiment my father has gotten up to this time.

What the hell just happened?

Adrian and Valentina shake our hands, and Ivan makes a joke about losing another one, which I don't understand.

I stare around at the rose petals, soft against my bare feet since we didn't have matching shoes to fit me. He did this for me? A whore? A nobody?

I just can't understand it.

Then the elevator dings.

Ivan stiffens in front of me, twisting to shove me behind him. Adrian does the same for Val. I wrestle his hand away to peer around the side of his bicep.

My father walks in like he was invited. "Well, this looks cozy."

22

IVAN

Arthur steps out of the elevator, wearing a black pinstripe suit. He's alone, which I think is fucking bold since he's come into Adrian's house, my domain, and expected to walk out alive. "Arthur, did you come to give yourself up as a wedding gift?"

His smile is polite but tense. "No, actually. I came to remind you of the terms of our deal and perhaps sweeten it a bit if it means lasting peace instead of a fragile one."

Then Arthur shifts his attention to Adrian and extends his hand. "I don't believe we've met before. I do believe you know who I am...as I know your name already as well. Thank you for inviting me to this lovely intimate ceremony. I'm so sorry I missed the official vows."

Adrian studies Arthur, dropping his hand after the initial shake. "I agreed to allow you to name your terms. I said nothing about an invitation."

Arthur's smile grows wider. "Well then, I guess I just have excellent timing."

My fingers are itching to go for the gun tucked into the waist of my pants. One bullet, and I can end it all. One bullet, and I can end this misery and shame.

Cilla curls her hand around my forearm, pulling herself from my shadow to stand beside me. "Father."

He matches her indifferent tone. "Daughter. Looks like you proved useful to me after all."

She stiffens beside me, only the tiniest amount, but I feel the tension in her grasp as she digs her fingernails into my jacket.

I start forward, but both she and Adrian hold me back.

Adrian releases me first. "Leave it for now. He wants to talk. We'll let him talk."

Val is wide-eyed, clutching her stomach as if she can protect it from this man and what he's done. I don't blame her one bit. I nod to Cilla. "Why don't you take Val to sit down. Your father, Adrian, and I can all have a little chat."

She quickly wraps an arm around Val's waist and leads her out of the room.

I turn to watch Arthur again. "You made a mistake coming here. I don't give a shit what kind of truce you think we have, but we don't. I don't want anything from you."

Arthur purses his lips and taps his chin in mock confusion for a second. "Oh, but I do believe you did want my daughter. Enough that you just married her. I'd say that's a hell of a lot if you'd rather bind yourself for life than turn her back over to me. Her loving father."

I clench my fists, and Adrian cuts his hand in front of me again. "No, don't engage, Ivan. He's trying to rile you up. Don't give him the satisfaction of seeing he's succeeded. It's not worth it."

I know he means the thing with the FBI. Fuck. Emmanuelle and Andrea. Whatever the hell happened there. Obviously, nothing good with Emmanuelle now in prison. Either way, Adrian is right. We are trying to keep out of the spotlight until the law enforcement's attention dies down again.

Arthur's gaze shifts unflinchingly to mine. "When you were my guest, I offered you a deal. My daughter in exchange for negotiating peace. You kept your end. I'm here, but you've decided to keep her, so we need to renegotiate."

Adrian shifts beside me, his own hands clenched, but nothing of the tension I can see in him is written on his face. "Well. It seems you're more like your brother than I was led to believe. Buying, selling, and bartering your own blood away for whatever you need."

"My brother is short-sighted and doesn't understand the firestorm he's crawled himself into. I do. I know who you are, Adrian Doubeck, and I know once you have a target, you won't stop until every member of my family is dead. I'm trying to save my little offshoot any way that I can. How can you fault me for that?"

I step closer to him. "I can fault you for anything I damn well please. The season is open motherfucker, and I'm coming for you."

Arthur narrows his eyes and shakes his head. "Ivan, please. The grown-ups are talking now. Why don't you run along and play with your new toy."

As if she heard him speaking about her, Cilla rushes back into the foyer, her bare feet slapping on the hardwood.

No one looks at her. I'm not taking my eyes off her father, and Adrian also knows to keep his eyes on the threat. Not that he'd be able to do much against both of us, but he doesn't take risks when Val is nearby. Not anymore.

Cilla curls her hand around my forearm again as if she might be able to step between us and hold me back. Why she'd bother to protect him, I don't know. Or maybe she'd do it thinking she's protecting me.

I focus on Adrian again. It's his order, even if this is my vengeance.

Adrian gives Arthur a nod. "Tell me your terms."

I go ramrod straight beside the man who's saved my life more than once. Hell, I've saved his more than once. We've been fighting side by side for years, and he'll listen to this asshole over me?

Never shifting his gaze from Adrian, Arthur nods in return. "I give you my brother and his entire male family line, and you let my little branch live. I don't have sons. The name will die when I do. I just don't intend to go out as soon as I'm sure he will."

Cilla squeezes my arm, and I glance down at her. Tears shimmer at the inner corners of her eyes. "Don't make a deal with him," she whispers. "He's never met a promise he didn't plan on breaking. That's not the words of a daughter speaking, just someone who knows him. He'll fail to deliver and then take off, change his name, and never be heard from again. He doesn't give a shit about our family name or lineage. He only cares about his experiments."

Arthur raises his hands in what I believe he thinks is a placating gesture. To me, he looks bored, like a teenager confronting a parent about a curfew. Cilla is right. He doesn't have the honor to keep his word, but I bet Adrian already realizes that. He reads people like others read books.

I pat Cilla's hand and shake my head so she doesn't give away anything else. Not protecting Arthur's secrets but protecting what we might know about him. Learn about him.

Focusing back on Arthur, I watch the exchange between him and Adrian. My friend is listening, but he's also calculating. I can see that as surely as Arthur can't. Because I know he wants every member of Arthur's family dead, including Arthur...he can't possibly make a deal to protect him when he promised his wife they'd be eradicated.

Arthur holds his hand out one more time for Adrian. "Think about it. We'll discuss."

I take a step forward, and Cilla grabs my elbow, trying to pull me back. She doesn't move me even an inch, of course. But the fact that she'd try pops a bubble inside my chest. Not exactly painful, but not a comfortable sensation either.

I glare down at her and shrug her off my arm. "Don't fucking touch me like that again."

Her eyes dart to Arthur, then to Adrian, and back to me. "I just…"

I turn, ignoring her, and focus on Arthur. "Get the fuck out, and don't come back unless I personally escort you inside this house."

He gives another mock nod and turns his back deliberately to wait for the elevator. My entire body is screaming at me to go after him. Push him down the stairs. Throw him out a window. Bash his brains into the side of a curb. Anything will be fine, really. As long as I don't have to hear another word out of his mouth again.

When the sight of him is gone, the elevator closed and descending, I face Cilla again. "Don't you dare get in my way like that again."

I grab her chin hard, forcing her head back so she meets my eyes. I don't give a shit if it's uncomfortable for her. This is a lesson she'll need to learn the hard way.

Adrian sighs beside me, then turns to leave. "I'll give you two newlyweds some privacy."

Then he's gone, and it's just us. I grip her tight enough to make her wince. "Let's go to my suite. We need to have a little chat about the rules."

23

CILLA

The second I opened my mouth, I knew I'd fucked up. He's been on edge about my father since the moment we got out of the compound. Counting down the minutes until he can kill him. And seconds after we are married...married to save my ass, I keep him from doing the one thing he's no doubt been dreaming of since the night he met me.

I try to pull my arm from his tight grip, but his hold is as iron as his will. Absolutely no give.

We get back to our suite in the penthouse, and the second the door closes, he releases my arm with a little shove.

I let him pace away, keeping my eyes on his back. Every few steps, he shifts farther and farther away from me in the room. I want to go to him, close the distance I can feel growing like a chasm between us, but I don't. If I get near him now, he might lash out, and things might get progressively worse.

He's not the first man I've met who has trouble controlling his temper. But he's the first man I've met who makes an effort to try, especially when it's at its worst.

I clear my throat loudly to get his attention. "Look, I'm sorry.

That was a stupid thing to do. I know I shouldn't have spoken my mind like that. I just…"

He rounds on me, his eyes narrowed to pinpricks of black. "You think I'm pissed because you spoke your mind? No. Fucking sass me all you want, in private. I'm pissed you did it in front of your father. If he spots a weakness, he'll strike, and right now, the only weakness he sees in me is you."

Ouch. I press my hand to my chest and try not to let him see how badly that stung. They only hit harder when they see how much they've hurt you. When they know exactly where to strike.

I drop my eyes and keep my mouth shut, but I've already opened things up, and I can feel his eyes on me, the warmth of him as he gets closer. The coward in me wants to shrink away and run, but that would only make things worse because he'd chase me. I know that now. He'd chase me, and the punishment for running would be so much worse than if I stayed. A tendril of heat curls through me at the idea, but I ignore it and my traitorous body. Now is not the time.

"You have anything else to add? Anything you didn't say in front of dear old daddy?" He almost spits in my face, he's so close now. I can smell mint on his breath and feel his heat so close. It takes all of my willpower not to melt into him. Beg forgiveness, offer him anything he wants if he doesn't just walk away from me right now and decide I'm not worth the effort.

He buries his face against my neck, and I squeeze my eyes closed as my heart sprints toward my rib cage. As he breathes me in, I do the same for him. Spicy and sweet at the same time. I lick my lips, dragging my bottom one in with my teeth. When he touches me, I lose control over myself, and I need to be able to stand here against his rage and not flinch, or he'll never trust me with it again. Never trust himself with me again.

I wrap my hands up, one over the back of his shoulder, the other around the curve at the nape of his neck. He leans in and pulls me toward him by my dress, his big hands fisted, one on either side. The way he grips me only throws gas on the fire that's a slow simmer in my gut. I'm already growing wet thinking about what he could do to me. How he would use me. How he would punish me. And I don't know if it's wrong. Or if it makes me a bad person, but I want it. All of it. I want his marks on my skin, teeth, hands, all of it.

Legally, I belong to him now, and I want the whole world to be able to see evidence of it. If his name is carved in deep, no one will be able to take that away from me. He'll be mine just as much as I'm his.

"If you need this," I whisper against his neck. "If you need this, I can handle it. I can handle anything you need. You can let yourself go."

He shakes his head over and over, but I can only feel his chin scuffing against my collarbone. "No. I can't let myself go because I'll hurt you. Everything between us can't be about my anger and pain."

I swallow the urge to beg. "What about my anger? What about my pain? Can it be about that? Give me this. Take my mind off my father so that all I'm thinking about is you."

His hands squeeze tighter, so his fingers dig into my waist, and the dress bunches between his hands and my body. "Don't tempt me like this, Malyshka. I'll hurt you. I can't live with myself if I hurt you."

I repeat the words I said to him before. The ones that still echo in my head when he looks at me. "If you need to hurt me, then hurt me. I can take it. More so, I want it. So much of the pain, the sex, the fear in my life has been about hurting me to see me break. To see me bend over and give in. But with you, it's different. You don't hurt me to break me. You hurt me to set me free, and I feel it in my bones. Please. Don't make me beg you. I will if that's what you want, but please…"

His head, lips, and his mouth come down on mine hard. He brings his hands up to cup my face to keep me still while his tongue thrusts between my lips. It's abrupt and brutal, and I love every second of it.

I go for his bowtie while he controls the kiss. The taste of him, the way he steers my face, using my head to steer my body at the same time, floods my system with the oblivion I'm craving.

Something has changed. The need for his touch is like a beat in my blood. Every pass of his fingers sends more moisture to my core. My pussy is already drenched, and he hasn't even taken my clothes off yet.

When he breaks the kiss, I'm dizzy and barely standing on my own two legs. All I can do is stare into his eyes.

"You don't want me gentle? Good. Because I've got punishment on my mind. I'm not going to fuck you until I dole that punishment out. Until you learn your lesson well enough not to question me in front of the others again."

I whimper. Both at the thought of him fucking me and whatever punishment his twisted mind might dream up. "What... what are you going to do to me?"

The corner of his mouth turns up in a smile that is meant to scare. It only makes me wetter.

"Take off your clothes and then lie across the edge of the bed, face down, ass up."

I swallow another noise, my fingers and toes tingling with the arousal coursing through me. I'm so turned on that nausea is making a slow roll through my belly. If he's not touching me in the next five seconds, I might go out of my mind.

I strip on the way to the bed, leaving my dress and panties where I remove them. When I reach the bed, I lie across the side, my front half supported by the bed, my feet on the floor. With such a big bed, I have to stand on my tiptoes to maintain the position but maybe being off balance is part of his plan.

There's no warning. A sharp pain rips across my upper thighs. I gasp and reach out to squeeze the covers. It takes a second to realize he just hit me with his belt. The stiff leather snaps across my skin in a painful arc. Another swat joins the other side, and heat burns down to my knees and up between my thighs.

His hand rubs across my stinging skin. "You like that, don't you. Tell me why?"

I'm on the edge of tears, but I can't let him see them yet. "Because it feels like forgiveness. Every hit is a new start. You punish me to forgive me, and that's all I want right now. I want you to forgive me, then I want you to fuck me."

"Can you take two more, Malyshka? Two more to brighten up your pretty skin, and then we'll forget the whole thing happened."

I swallow a lump in my throat and nod, my face turned to the side as the tears leak down my cheeks. "Yes, please."

The pain streaks across my ass this time, and I almost lose my footing. He catches me around the hips, and I blink as pleasure follows the pain. At some point, he removed his pants, and all I feel is the hot brand of his hard cock pressing into the seam of my ass. He's still wearing his boxer briefs, but I don't care. The contact is enough to make me push back against him.

"Last one, then I'll give you what you want. Is this how you imagined your wedding night? My marks on your skin, maybe my cum streaking over the welts?"

I can't breathe, my stomach churns, and my pussy is so wet it's already clenching on empty air needing him to fill me up.

His last hit comes after a few seconds. Pain burns across the other cheek of my ass, and my entire hindquarters stings, burns, and blazes from his punishment. The belt hits the floor with a clink, and I open my eyes to catch movement behind me and the rustle of his clothing.

Then heaven as he shoves inside me in one long smooth thrust. I'm soaked, and there's no resistance. I relax back into him and let him take charge of my hips.

"You're so beautiful like this. Seeing all this snowy white skin with my marks makes me want to tattoo my name across every inch of it. So no one, not even you, can doubt who you belong to."

I clutch the covers, my orgasm already rising up. Each thrust into me hits the welts on my legs and ignites the fire all over again.

"Fuck. Fuck. Fuck. Fuck. Fuuuccckk." I'm chanting it as he fucks me faster and faster. Each slam of his powerful thighs against me amps me higher. I don't even need stimulation on my clit to get there this time. Only a few more strokes, and I'm going to fall into the most powerful orgasm of my life.

His voice wraps around my throat, holding tight. "Wait for me, Cilla. Wait for me to come. If you don't, we'll do this again until you can be a good girl and wait for me."

He picks up his pace, pounding into me so hard he has to lift my hips up to give himself the angle he wants. I don't care. He can use every inch of me if he lets me come soon.

"Please," I beg. "Please. Please. Please."

"Now, angel. Do it now. Come for me. I want you to milk this out of me. You earned every drop of my cum inside you. So take it."

He slams into me again, and I shatter. It's oblivion on a razor's edge. Where pleasure and pain meet and mingle in a way only a few can really understand. When he squeezes me tighter and slams into me one more time, I can feel that hot jet of him deep inside me. His groan is obscene and turns me on all over again.

I let my eyes drift closed in the aftermath, and I sleep without nightmares for the first time in years.

24

IVAN

*I*n the morning, I wake early, the sun barely glinting through the windows. Cilla lies on her stomach beside me, one leg tucked up so her knee juts out almost over the edge of the bed. Her hands are tucked under her pillow, and her ass and thighs are still faintly pink from her punishment.

It wasn't the wedding night I had ever imagined. Not that I'd imagined any kind of long-term relationship. I figured I'd be dead by thirty. The victim of my own reckless anger and an impromptu overreaction.

I carefully climb out of bed, arranging the blankets to cover her bare thighs. While I dress, I keep my eyes on her. Yesterday was stressful for her, so I want her to stay in bed and rest for now.

In my usual white button-down and black slacks, I head toward the command center to find Kai.

Facing the wall of computers on the far side of the large round table, he leans back in a chair, his jacket off, vest unbuttoned, sleeves rolled up. In his mouth, he's rolling around a lollipop while he types at a furious pace at the keyboard on his lap.

I wait until he notices me, so I don't cause him to lose his spot. When his fingers slow, and he glances up at me, he tugs the lollipop from his lips. "Shouldn't you be in bed...with your wife?"

I flip him off and face his screens. "What are you doing?"

He hits a few keys, clearing away coding screens to reveal a map. "It's a diagram of the city where we've seen strange occurrences of drugs. Or rather strange drug sales."

"Can you do any research on local chemists? Professors or working chemists who might be helping Arthur with his business?"

Kai shift in the chair and resettles his feet up on the table, pushing him back in the chair. I keep my eyes on the screen while he types away, searching through whatever he searches for to find the answers.

While he's typing, he says, "I'm a little worried about you, man."

I don't even justify his statement with a look. "Go mama bear one of the twins, Kai. I don't need you to worry about me."

"The twins have each other to lean on. You don't let yourself lean on anyone."

I face him, my eyes narrowed. "And who do you lean on, Kai?"

"Adrian. My sisters. I have people in my life. You might have Priscilla now, but I'd bet my favorite suit you don't open up to her."

"Why would I? This is a marriage of convenience. It's a way to keep her safe. I don't need to open up to the woman who helped kidnap and keep me hostage."

Kai continues to type, the sound of clacking filling the room. I don't understand how he can think with the racket he makes.

Maybe I should get him some noise-canceling headphones for Christmas. Or myself some if I have to stay in this room much longer.

"Are you going to grill me or search for what I asked?"

Kai bites down, crunching on his lollipop. "Calm the fuck down, man. You're the one who asked me to do this. It's not a fucking Google search. Give me a minute."

Needing to justify…something…I keep watching the screen. "You would do the same if you were in my shoes. Hell, you killed anyone involved in holding you. Why is it when I do the same thing, somehow something to worry about?"

We lapse into silence while Kai executes his search. I don't need to talk about things, and usually, neither does Kai. Maybe everyone pairing off into relationships has made the team soft. Although, once upon a time, I would swear nothing could soften Adrian from the rigid stone statue his father created him to be.

Kai continues his work, and eventually, I grab a cup of coffee from the machine at the far end of the room. While I sip the hot liquid, Kai types, and types, and types some more. It all looks like gibberish to me, but I know he's good at what he does. I might have a few contacts on the street, but I wouldn't trust anyone else with this research.

I swallow a wave of guilt, pull out a chair beside Kai, and sit to watch him work. We stay silent, and that's fine for both of us. After a while, he prints a list and slides it down the table to me.

I catch the paper and read the four names aloud. Four chemists who could have some involvement in Arthur's activities. "This is perfect, thank you."

When I head toward the door, Adrian enters before I make it. Alexei follows close behind him. Since they are in my way, I have to stand there and wait.

Adrian gives me a once-over and then waves Alexei up to stand beside him. "I want you to take him with you, Ivan. He can help, and you need an extra hand. Either for security or running around doing whatever you don't need to be seen doing."

I bite the inside of my lip until I taste blood, so I don't let my anger get the better of me. "Fine, but he takes orders from me, not you, and not Kai."

Alexei smiles, a dimple digging deep into each cheek. He looks like a fucking walking Abercrombie and Fitch ad. In a suit. A prep in a fucking suit. "Just don't smile so much, and make sure you're ready when I am. What about Andrea? Will she be okay?"

The smile slips off Alexei's face real quick. "She's fine, and if she hears you asking after her like she can't take care of herself, then she's going to kick your ass, and I'll enjoy watching it."

I give him one last glare, ignoring Adrian since I don't want to get pummeled today, and walk out.

But Kai chases after me when I'm not two feet out the door, leaving all four of us in the middle of the damn hall. Any of the women could hear us out here. "For fuck's sake, if you have more to say, at least go back into the command center where no one can walk by and overhear us."

It takes a second for us all to shuffle back inside. Alexei hangs back out of all our way. I glare at Kai. "Did you need something else?"

Kai drags his gaze from Adrian's to mine. "I know you went to see Eric. We want to keep this as low-key as possible."

Heat erupts in my belly, forcing me to clench my fists to calm the hell down. "I'm aware of our current difficulties and what we should and shouldn't be involved in at the moment. Thank you for the reminder." I grit my teeth the entire time I speak.

"Watch your tone," Adrian snaps. "He's only trying to keep all of us safe. We know the council likes to attack when it gets cornered. It's only a matter of time before it comes at us, and I don't intend to be in the crosshairs. Hell, I don't want Valentina and our child anywhere near that fucking mess."

He's right to remind me that this isn't a fight that stays with me. Once one of us gets involved in something, all of us are. Everyone needs to do what they can to make sure Valentina stays safe.

Some of my anger fades, and I nod. "I'm sorry. I get it, and I know. I'm not trying to be a massive dickhole here, but I'm having a hard time thinking about what they did to me and what they've done to her."

None of them need me to clarify that I mean Cilla. She's the person who has lived with Arthur her entire life. The fact that she kept herself alive all this time means she's the strongest person I've ever met. I intend to make sure she stays safe too. But at what cost? Would I give up Adrian or Val's safety to make that happen?

A week ago, I'd have gutted someone for even suggesting it. Now, after knowing the warmth of her arms. After feeling her compassion, I'm not so sure.

I hang my head, my shame no doubt apparent in my eyes if I look at my friends. "I need to go check on her. Make sure she's okay after last night."

Kai nudges me with his elbow. "What? Did you wear out your new bride already? You have to give her some time to adjust."

He's trying to break the tension, and it works. I hammer him back with my fist in his ribs. He doubles over and then shoves me away.

Adrian sighs. "Children. We were discussing an important topic. You can save the grab ass for later. Get back to business."

He's right. I sober and put a little more distance between all of us. "I'm sorry. I'll be sure that nothing comes back on our family."

It's enough for Adrian by the nod he gives me. Kai matches it. Then Alexei comes around and heads out the door before me. "I'll wait for you to text me that you need something. But if I don't hear from you at least once a day, I'll assume the worst and go into full guerilla mode."

I shove his shoulder hard enough to send him off balance. "Do you even know what that word means?"

"Shut up, asshole. You aren't that much older than I am."

His easygoing nature makes me smile. At least one of us hasn't been ruined by the world yet. I hope his twin gets her own quick smile back in the future too. Way more than any of us have been willing to give has already been stolen from us. By society. By our own flesh and blood. I don't intend to make it easy for them to break Cilla as well.

25

CILLA

The move back to his safehouse apartment feels like a retreat. From the moment we arrive, Ivan seems to withdraw. I'm not sure what happened between when he woke up and when we left, but I don't think it was good. Not that he's going to open up to me about it.

Each day he grows more and more angry. At first, I thought it was because of me and how I trapped him into this marriage. Hell, he wouldn't be here now if it weren't for me and what happened with my father.

I don't have high hopes. Once he kills Arthur, I expect he'll ask for a divorce, but a tiny part of me wants to keep him a little longer. But would he hate me for it?

So while we are here, I try to keep myself busy. Try to, being the operative word. When I try to clean, he stops me, saying he pays people to do it. When I try to cook, he shoos me out of the kitchen and says we can order from the restaurant down the street. Even when I try to touch him, he traps my hand against his chest and shakes his head.

I don't know what I did to change things between us, but I

can't take it much longer. He's like a ghost. An angry poltergeist who can't let go of his unfinished business. I just don't know how to fix things between us.

A week after the wedding, after five days of being cooped up, I've had enough. I didn't try to gain my freedom to be locked up in a prettier cage. It's afternoon when I find him at a bench in his armory, cleaning his weapons. An array of tiny parts is laid out on the table in front of him, all perfectly lined up, while he polishes one part with a stained off-white cloth.

"What are you doing in here?" His voice is gruff, and he doesn't even glance my way.

I wouldn't say he scares me, but I'm wary of sparking his anger. "Is this what you do in your free time?"

He keeps polishing the already shiny part in his hands. "I don't have free time."

As he's been for days, it's a testy answer. "Okay, fine. Is this something you enjoy doing?"

His eyes finally flash up to mine. "Watch your tone."

I sigh. What the hell can I do to get through to him? "I'm trying to get to know you if you haven't noticed."

Now he lifts his head to look at me, really look at me. "Why?"

Shit. I can't tell him the truth—that I've developed feelings for my husband, and I want to know more about him. So I shrug. "What else is there to do here but talk. I'm bored out of my mind, and you make a good distraction."

He narrows his eyes and sweeps my body with his gaze. "A distraction, huh?"

I reach out to pick up one of the parts, but he slaps the back of my hand before I can clutch anything. "Sorry. I just mean, we are stuck together for a while. Maybe we can get to know one another."

"What if I don't want to know anything about you?" Unlike his previous statements, there's nothing cold in his tone. He says it flat, dull, like it's a conditioned response used to push people away and not his true feelings.

Or maybe I just want it to be that way. I want him to want me as much as I want him, and so far...he doesn't. It hurts that he doesn't need me like I need him.

I shrug like it doesn't matter, even as a new kind of pain blooms inside my chest. It's been a long time since someone had the power to hurt me. A very long time since I'd given anyone that power. Somehow, I'd given it to Ivan. The gruff, tattoo-covered bastard is determined to save me even though he doesn't even like me.

I'm so fucked.

Instead of continuing the conversation and inviting more pain, I spin and head back out the door. I wish I hadn't gone in there to begin with. What the hell did I think I was going to do? Get him to open up and tell me about his terrible childhood? Share my own pain, and we'd connect, and he'd finally take me back to bed where we belong?

I wander into the living room and walk up to the windows to stare out. It's a dreary day, gray overhead with a low cloud bank hiding some of the view beyond the immediate buildings. Maybe I'll be out there soon. He'll get tired of playing protector and send me off on my own. That's what I want anyway, right?

There's a knock on the door. I spin, my heart and lungs and fucking spleen in my throat. Did he find us already? Is the peace over so soon? I don't want to run anymore, and I can't stand to see Ivan get hurt again.

I square my shoulders, readying to throw myself on anyone's mercy to ensure nothing happens to him. He kept me safe, and I can do the same for him if it comes down to it.

Ivan wanders out, wiping his hands on his cloth. He's only wearing slacks, and a button-down dress shirt, with the sleeves pushed up. Somehow even with all that oil and grease, his white shirt doesn't have a spot on it.

He glances at me as I stand tense near the windows. "It's fine. It's just Alexei. No one is going to find you here. You trust that, right?"

I swallow and don't answer. He waits a moment, then crosses to open the door.

A man I saw before slips in and locks it behind him. He's holding an oversized cream envelope and passes it to Ivan.

Alexei nods to me and heads to the bar without a word.

Ivan rips the top of the envelope and pulls out something. "Fuck. He's not serious, is he?"

I'm already crossing to his side and immediately spot the names on the invitation. "Is that from Adrian?"

Ivan shoots me a look that says, really? "Adrian wouldn't send this. If he wanted to throw a party for us, he'd tell me himself. This is from your father." He passes me the envelope. "Apparently, he wants to celebrate our marriage in front of the entire society."

Alexei joins us, sipping on something in a low-ball glass. Whiskey by the smell of it. "Adrian got this this morning, sent me to check if it was real, and then delivered it here."

Ivan studies his friend, and I can't help but stare between them, trying to see anything either might give away.

"He's definitely having a party. I'm not sure how many people will attend, but he's accessed society's caterers and vendors. The ones everyone usually uses." His shoulders sag a bit. "I didn't get much on the guest list, though. There wasn't one published anywhere that I could bribe or steal."

Ivan clutches his shoulder while he scans the invitation again. "You did fine. Thank you for bringing this over so quickly. We obviously aren't going, but I want to make sure we know what he's planning; if he's planning something other than simple gloating."

Alexei sips his drink and throws his tall frame down on a coach. "You sure that's a good idea? Not attending, I mean. He'll want to gloat…look here at my new shiny connection to the Doubeck family. He might have important people there, people you'll want access to."

Ivan glances at me. "Would he be that stupid?"

I shrug. "He's vain and loves looking like he's on top of the world, on top of everything, so yes, but it would be more about vanity and social standing than business for him."

I keep my eyes on Ivan as he considers. He stares at the invitation in his hands, clutching it so tightly that I think he's resisting the urge to ball it up and toss it away. If he doesn't do it soon, I'll do it for him. This feels like a trap, and having the invitation here, in a place that is supposed to be safe, makes things feel bad…spoiled…and I don't know how to fix it. This is the first place I've felt truly safe. The first time I've slept in a real bed for a very long time.

Ivan skips his eyes to my face and then over to Alexei behind me. "We need to shop. She'll need some clothes."

It takes me a second to figure out what he's saying. "Are you talking about me? Why do I need clothes?" I pluck at the soft sweater leggings combo I'm wearing. An outfit given to me by Val. Along with several others. "I have clothes. Val gave me more than I need."

He draws me in, hands framing my hips, one of them still clutching the invitation. I close my eyes at the intimate touch. "Go get your shoes on."

I don't put up a fight, and I do what he asks. Only because he touched me and softened for the first time in days.

Alexei comes with us but trails behind more like a bodyguard than a friend. Inside the shop, Alexei speaks to the shopkeeper, and she rushes off to empty the store. Did people really do that? "This isn't necessary."

Ivan drops his eyes to mine, lips thin, and shakes his head. I swallow and nod, recognizing the look in his eyes.

When the shopkeeper comes over, her eyes taking in all of Ivan and heating, he dips his head and whispers in her ear.

I swallow the hot fizz of jealousy that sparks inside me. We might be married, but he's made it clear this week that it's in name only. If he wants to fuck her right here, there's very little I can do about it.

She heads off in a rush and returns with a cart of clothing on hangers. Then leaves. Alexei and Ivan thumb through the clothing, pulling dresses off the rack. Occasionally, they'd look at me, assess me, then go back to their work. I have no patience for this shit.

After what feels like an eternity, I go toward the shop windows and stare at the bookstore across the street. I don't read much, I didn't get the chance growing up, so maybe it's why I love books. But because I love them, I can never have them. It was always one more thing my father could use to hurt me.

When Ivan is satisfied with his selections, he leaves Alexei to handle the final arrangements. He stands beside me with his hands in his pockets. "Do you want to go in there?"

I shake my head and swallow hard. "No. I'm fine. We should get back. It's still not safe, right, not while my father can get to us?"

He raises an eyebrow. "I doubt he's waiting in the bookstore to pop out and murder us in the biography section."

He takes my arm, gripping my upper bicep, and hauls me out the door, across the street, and into the other store. To anyone else, I might look like a petulant child being dragged along. But I feel the care he uses as he grips me, the softness to his much wider step, so I don't stumble. He leads me deep into the store. "Pick what you want but be quick. I want to leave as soon as Alexei is done paying."

I start in the fantasy section even though I find the huge tomes intimidating. But they are huge and give me so many pages to savor. I grab two books with colorful covers and go find Ivan.

He closes the screen of his phone when he spots me. "That's it? No."

I fumble after him as he enters the aisle again. He takes a second to check what I'd grabbed and then selects five more books.

Five more books I don't have room to pack if I run. "I can't pay for this. And I don't have room for it."

He says nothing as he leads me to the register, pays, and then takes my hand to head back to the car.

Once we are tucked inside, he stares out the window while Alexei drives. "You need to learn you are my wife. You want nothing. You need nothing. And you take anything you want. When you understand that, we'll be on the same page. Until then...I won't be able to give you what you want."

26

IVAN

She's the most beautiful woman I've ever seen in my life. Standing at the mirror, she smoothes the folds of the blood-red dress I picked out for her. Her eyes are wide and too bright behind the makeup she's already applied. I take her in, her scent, and let myself relax. I'm going to need that tonight.

I'm content to watch her, but she doesn't like the loaded silence. "Alexei has good taste."

I make a noise of agreement. She doesn't need to know I picked this dress specifically because of how I want to peel her out of it later. It's better that I don't since things have gotten more complicated between us than I anticipated, but I can't help the desire to at least see her in it. The dress molds to her curves and then flares out at the bottom, giving her hourglass shape even more obscene proportions.

When I can pull my eyes away, I adjust my already perfect bowtie and meet her eyes in the mirror. "Ready?"

"Do we have to go? Will we gain anything by giving my father exactly what he wants?"

I turn her to face me and scan her features. "We don't have

anything to lose. Best case, we learn something, and I can kill everyone. Worst case, I just kill everyone."

Her eyes are wide and starting to brim with tears. "You don't..."

I tilt her chin and stare at her full, bright red lips. I desperately want to kiss her, but I don't want to mess up the makeup she took her time applying. "I'm not planning to kill anyone, at least tonight."

She sags against me, using my chest to balance her weight. "Okay. Okay. That's good. Yes, let's get this over with so we can get out of these clothes."

I pull a necklace from my pocket, a loaner from Adrian, even though I could have bought one myself, and gently slip it around her neck. It sparkles in the bright bathroom lights, and she runs her fingers over it. "Wow. It's so pretty."

It would be easier to keep my thoughts to myself, but I can't help it. Not with her looking so delicious and me being a starving man. "Not as beautiful as you. Let's go."

The party has already started when we arrive. Thankfully, I got to miss the awkward mingling when things are just getting going. The room is packed, but I don't recognize anyone here. I lean down to pull her into my side. "Do you recognize anyone?"

She's shivering, and I tighten my grip around her waist. "Malyshka, you have to calm down, or I won't be able to stay calm. You know what happens when I lose my calm. Where are we? Have you ever lived here?"

It takes effort. I watch as she resettles her shoulders and pastes a fake smile on her face. "No, this is likely his girlfriend's house. Or something. Or maybe he has houses everywhere that I didn't know about since I lived at the compound."

The idea he made her live in some hovel when he had this place with its crystal-cut chandeliers and silk curtains ignites my rage to murder him even more.

"Oh, I'm so happy you two love birds could attend." His voice from behind me makes me stiffen. I stare down into Cilla's face and wrestle with my control. It would be nothing to pull out my gun and blow this jackass a new asshole. The season ends very soon, but it's not over yet. I still have time.

"Please," Cilla whispers, her hand gripping my forearm hard enough that it allows me to focus. I inhale her clean soapy scent deeply and then turn to stand beside her, facing Arthur.

He's dressed like a villain from a damn Agatha Christie adaptation with a silk jacket and ascot. It makes him look twenty years older than he probably is. "I'm so glad you got my invitation. If you tell me where you're making your home, I can send the invites directly next time."

He holds his hand out to shake, but I ignore it, slipping my free hand into my pocket. "Sending anything care of the penthouse is just fine."

Arthur smiles like the slight is nothing, then waves a server over to offer drinks. I give him a dead-eyed stare. "I'll decline. I hope you understand."

Cilla's hold tightens, and she refuses a drink as well. Did he think we'd walk right back into his clutches and trust he won't drug us just because he has a deal with Adrian?

When we all stare at each other in silence, Arthur smiles wide and moves off toward another set of guests. Cilla sags and lets out a long sigh beside me. "You didn't kill him. We are doing great. How long do we have to stay here?"

Arthur laughs loudly from across the room, and I catch him mentioning Adrian's name. Of course, he'd try to use his new connections to gain favors or more patrons. Let's go to the bar and get a drink. There are likely people here he won't want to drug.

While we stand at the bar, I pull out my phone and snap

pictures. They are set up to automatically upload to Kai so he can identify them all.

A text comes through, and I open it.

THE WOMAN beside the window is my sister, Julia. Find out what the fuck she is doing there.

I STARE AROUND and spot the girl on the far side of the room. Same warm tan skin as Kai, same silky black hair as Selena, but she's a little thinner, and she stands a bit more rigid than both of them. The silver sequin dress she's wearing hugs her tall thin frame tightly, and I think I spot the strap of a sheath at her thigh.

I lead Cilla with me since I'm not willing to leave her alone. We stop at Julia's elbow. "Julia?"

She turns to look at me but doesn't register any recognition. "Yes? Are you looking for me?"

I study her face and the blank look in her eyes. "Are you okay? Do you need help? Kai sent me over here to talk to you."

She stares around the room. "My brother? How would he even know I'm here. How do you know him?"

Without giving her our entire history, I keep it simple. "We work together, and he's one of the few people I'd count as a friend."

Now she smiles, and I see the resemblance to her brother even more. "He does like to collect interesting friends. Tell him I said hello."

Then without another word, she drifts into the crowd. I try to keep my eyes on her, but the room is growing fuller, especially as people drift off to the large empty room for dancing.

"Why was Kai's sister here?" Cilla asks, drawing my attention.

I shake my head and study the crowd around us, snapping more pictures to send to Kai. "I have no idea. She is in a related field to us, not your father, so I'm not sure why she'd be here. Maybe she has a target here."

Cilla shapes the word. "Target?"

"We'll talk about it later. Do you see anyone you recognize? Anyone Kai should research?"

Her shoulders sink as she takes in the other partygoers. "I recognize a few guards from the compound but no one else. Maybe a few people who have come to the casino while I worked there."

The reminder of how she sold her body to get to me jolts something loose inside my chest. Fuck. We need to get on a different subject before I start hunting down her old clients.

"Let's dance for a moment, and then we can get out of here. Stay long enough that he feels satisfied. I think I've got enough photos for Kai to use in his research." I lead her to join the other dancers, thankful for the distance the action gives me from the others roaming around. I fucking hate parties. All of them. The only reason I ever attend is to make sure Adrian stays protected.

She falls into step like she's a natural. I pull her close and enjoy the way the feel of her calms something in my soul. Will it last forever? I have no idea, but for right now, I'll take it.

For a few moments, I let us dance in silence and enjoy this. We don't get things like this very often, if ever, so we should savor them while we have them.

Her hands squeeze the back of my jacket, and I close my eyes. It's a risk. If Arthur sees how much I need this, he'll use it against me. When I open my eyes, she's staring up at me, a softness on her face. Arthur might not have seen it, but Cilla does.

When the song ends, I lead her off the dance floor. Arthur wastes no time coming over again, an even bigger smile on his face. "Might I have a moment to speak with my daughter?"

I'm about to tell him to fuck off when Cilla shakes her head and steps forward. "We won't go far, and then you and I can go home."

They move a few feet away. I can't hear them over the crowd, but I can see she really doesn't want to speak to him. If her posture gets any more rigid, I will march across the room, drag her into my arms, and carry her out of here. Every time he speaks, she almost flinches until there is a good foot of space between them.

My patience is up. I can't let him keep hurting her, and whatever he is saying is definitely hurting her. If it's on purpose, I'm going to fucking slit his throat.

I cut through the crowd, not caring who I bump into or who I have to push out of my way to get there.

Arthur goes silent and shoots me a grin as I approach. "Oh, I think Cilla might be ready to leave. But before you go, might I have a word with you too?"

I push Cilla behind me and then point toward the door. "Alexei is waiting right outside the door. Go to him and wait for me. I'll be there in a second."

I focus down on Arthur's grinning face. "You speak to her again. I kill you. You put that wounded dog look in her eyes. I kill you. You so much as breathe wrong in her direction, I will fucking slit your throat and feed you to a pack of dogs."

He smiles more. "You have dogs? How interesting."

"No. I don't. But if you push me, I'll get some and raise them to crave the taste of your blood specifically. Don't fuck with me, Arthur. I have very little patience when it comes to you."

He sips his champagne, seemingly unconcerned. "And why is that? We have an agreement, or at least, your employer and I do."

"Then you better keep your side of the deal before we run out of patience completely. Adrian isn't famous for patience. He might be well known for beating a man to death, but definitely not his patience."

Arthur sets his drink on the counter and pulls the edges of my jacket together as if he's straightening my suit. "Before you decide to kill me, you should know how much my little girl there is using you. How much she's acting on my behalf and how much she's acting on her own."

I flinch, and he smiles, knowing he has hit the mark. I turn my back when he releases my jacket and head to the door. I can't wait to shoot that bastard in the head, and if Cilla has betrayed me, she'll join her father in the ground.

27

CILLA

Something changed. I don't know if it was at the party in general or if my father said something to him as we left, but the ride back to the apartment is tense. He may have been distant before, but not like this. It's like he's put up a brick wall between us, and the second I try to climb over, there are death lasers ready to take me out.

So we sit in silence, and at the apartment, more silence. But where the car felt tense, this feels...explosive.

I rip off my heels and toss them over by the couch so I can be flat on my feet when I go to him. It takes me a few minutes to get the courage to approach.

He stands on the far side of the room, staring out the window, his back and shoulders pushed back and rigid. My father had to have said something to him. But what? Why antagonize Ivan when he's so close to getting what he wants.

I cross to stand to his left and stare out at the dark sky. The lights in the other towers twinkle around us, looking like another universe. "Are you okay?"

"Don't speak." His voice is like ice.

I wrap my arms around my middle to give myself the courage to stand my ground. But I do as he asks and keep my mouth shut.

The urge to touch him is a chant in my head. I want to reach out and soothe whatever damage my father has done in the few words he spoke to him. When I can no longer resist, I reach out my right hand and brush the back of his shoulder.

He explodes, knocking my hand away with one arm, his other coming up to cup my neck and walk me back to the window. The entire world at my back.

His face is pink, and his eyes are rimmed with raw anger and pain. "How could I have been so stupid? Have you been playing me this entire time? Was it all a game to you? Come in here, get under my skin, and give me something in my life to finally hope for?"

I wrap my hands around his wrist, holding on even though he's not hurting me, just holding me. Hot tears slide down my cheeks. "Is that what he said to you? That I'm what...here because he sent me? Do I have that right? You're only stupid if you believe him."

He leans down, his face an inch from mine. "You're good. Really. You almost had me. All it took was me considering why in the hell you would want someone like me to begin with. You're...you wouldn't look twice at me under normal circumstances."

A sob falls from my lips, and I have to close my eyes to clear the tears. "What are you talking about? All it took was one word from him to make you doubt me...after all we've been through?"

My heart is breaking, cracking open, and shattering into tiny pieces. I sob, leaning my head back against the wall as he pins me. He asks how he could have been stupid; I'm feeling the same thing right this second. I knew better than to let my heart get involved. Hell, I actively tried not to let it, yet here I am, having it broken. After so many years of protecting myself from every abuse, maybe my father has finally won. He's finally broken me; all it took was using someone else to do it.

I open my eyes, and he's blurry through the tears. "I don't care what you think. This wasn't some kind of setup. If he told you that, then he's trying to get between us. He must have seen that I care about you. Now he's trying to get his revenge against me after all these years of not giving him the zombie-like submissive he's always wanted in a daughter."

I feel dead inside. The earth was dug up and salted where my heart used to be. He squeezes my neck and leans in closer, so close I can almost taste him on my lips. Despite my emotions, my body still craves him like nothing I've ever felt.

He doesn't say anything, just looks into my face, sweeping his gaze over my lips, up to my eyes, and back down again. Over and over.

I try to pry his hand loose, but he doesn't budge. "If you think I've betrayed you, then let me go. You can just kill me and be done with it." Maybe, at least, he can give me that kindness.

"Oh no, if you've betrayed me, you'll pay for that mistake before I kill you."

The rope of my patience snaps, and I dig my nails into his hand. "No. You don't get to stand there and act like you're the one who was wronged. What can you possibly do to me that wasn't already done before? You want to rape me…fine. You want to cut my skin and watch me bleed…been there…done that too. You want to hurt me until I pass out from the pain? Guess what, still won't be the first. The only thing you could do was be the first to break my heart. And you just did, so congratulations. I didn't think a new way to hurt me existed, but you managed to find it. Great job."

His forehead crinkles as he studies me, his fingers tightening a fraction. "I'm only going to ask you this one time. Was everything that has happened since we broke out of your father's compound a lie?"

Part of me wants to spit in his face, fight, kick, slap him. But I've been down that road before, and it only ends in more pain and more recovery for me later. I hold tight to my anger and continue to claw at his hand. He doesn't even flinch. "No. Everything that's happened since I left my father's compound has been the only real life I've ever lived. Don't you see that? I'd rather die than betray you, especially to him."

My words hang between us, and he slowly loosens his grasp and drops his hand. Even if he believes me, the damage is done. I can't even look at him without seeing the hate in his eyes, the desire to watch me bleed. Not out of pleasure but in pain.

He reaches out, but I slap his hand away. "Fuck you. You don't get to stand here and treat me like shit, then touch me afterward. I don't know what was happening between us, and I'm sure as hell not going to tell you how I feel—felt—but you broke it. You ruined it. Or I guess my father did. He's finally won. I'm done fighting."

I squeeze out from between him and the windows and head to the bedroom, needing space between us. Could I walk away from him? No, even if I wanted to, I couldn't run. He's the only tether I have left on Earth. The only thing I want for myself. But I have to figure out how to forgive him first.

Glass shatters behind me as I close the door, strip out of the fancy dress, and drop it on the floor. I sit on the side of the bed naked, just breathing, trying to stop the tears from rolling down my cheeks.

There's another crash from the other room, but I can't bring myself to go to him, to comfort him and take away that anger. Not when it's his fault there's this massive hole in my chest.

I don't know how much time passes, but the door to the bedroom opens. I glance up and spot the blood first, dripping off his fingers, his arm, and his face in tiny cuts. The bedside lamp makes it possible for me to see all the damage. What the hell did he do to himself?

He's quiet when he comes closer and quieter still when he sinks to his knees in front of me. His face is carefully blank even though his eyes are red, and he's dripping blood all over the off-white carpets.

So very gently, he slides his hands up my thighs, leaving a smear of blood on my pale skin. "How could you ever want a monster like me?" His voice is a ragged whisper. "You're beautiful, sexy, and so very kind. It hurts to even look at you. So it took nothing to make me doubt because I am nothing, and you are everything. I didn't realize how much I needed you until I saw the same emptiness I feel every day entering your eyes."

I can't look at him, so I stare down at the smears of blood on my legs, the cuts and nicks on his tattooed arms and hands. His cuff links are gone, and his shirt sleeves hang off him at the forearm, all stained with blood.

I carefully run a finger over one of the shallow cuts. He hisses, and I look up into his eyes. "What did you do to yourself?"

"It's nothing. It will heal. But will we?"

"I don't know," I whisper. "It's like everything you said ripped out some vital part of me I needed to feel. Now there's nothing but an empty hole. Maybe I like it better that way."

"No," he growls. He leans up, sliding his hands to the bed beside my legs and getting in my face so I lean back.

He settles his still-clothed weight over my naked one. "You say you can't feel, but it's self-preservation."

His teeth settle over my pulse point, and my body jerks like he's put a defibrillator on my chest. I sure as shit felt that.

He bites harder until the pleasure-pain point shifts more and more to pain. I shove at his chest, and he barely loosens his hold on me.

When he finally lifts his head, I'm breathing heavily, the pain sparking along my body underneath his.

"Don't let him win. I almost did. Don't let him beat you."

I blink and stare at the ceiling. When he slides his hand down my stomach, I feel the warmth of his fingers and the wet trickle of blood on his fingertips as he opens my body, plunging his fingers deep.

I don't know if it's his nearness or my body just lights up when he's around, but I'm already wet, and between that and his own blood, he slides two fingers inside me easily. "Do you feel that?"

I nod.

"No. Tell me you feel it. Say it."

Swallowing hard, I nod again. "I feel it."

He curls his fingers inside me, touching a spot that makes me jump, then my body hum. "Oh, you felt that, didn't you, Malyshka? Don't worry, I'll make it so good for you. Just for you tonight."

He pumps his fingers in as he scrapes his teeth down the side of my neck. I tighten my muscles against him, wanting more, needing more. He's right, I feel it, and I'm terrified of losing it all again. "Please."

"You don't have to beg me for this." He slides his hand from my body, gently parts my thighs, and kneels between them. His bare head, haloed in tattoos, kneeling with his face an inch from my pussy, is enough to push me headlong toward orgasm. My whole body contracts just looking at him.

He uses his thumbs to pull my folds apart, then leans forward and sucks my clit into his mouth. I arch off the covers and grab onto the back of his head, needing grounding. He bites gently, then sucks again, sending shock waves of pleasure through my system. When he sucks a third time, I come in great gasping breaths. His hands grip my thighs so tightly I'll have bruises.

When he lifts his face to look at me, I stare down at him. "Don't fucking hurt me like that again."

"So you forgive me?"

I narrow my eyes. "It's going to take more than you eating me out to earn my forgiveness."

A smile starts at the corner of his lips, bloody and jagged from the cuts on his face. "Then I guess I better get started."

28

IVAN

Two days later, when Adrian calls to tell me Arthur is ready to hold up his end of the deal, I still feel like a raw open wound. I let him get to me, and that feels like I've let him in somehow. For a second, I let him do exactly what he planned and ruined whatever had begun between Cilla and me.

Now, all I want is to see his blood run between my fingers. Even more than before, I imagine putting my knife to his throat and giving him that one final deadly smile.

If I voice these desires to Priscilla, she'll try to talk me out of it. Well, maybe.

Since the night of the party, she's different. Colder. Quieter, and it kills something inside me that I did that to her. That I have her feeling unsafe around me for even a second.

I slide a plate of food across the table to her. It's nothing more than a huge heaping plate of mixed fruit, one of her favorites for breakfast, but she merely picks at it. "Do we have to see him again? What if Adrian or Kai handles the end of the deal? It was made with them, after all."

As much as I wish I could give her this, I can't, not after what

Sal's family, her family, did to mine. We all need to be there to witness the end of it. "I'm sorry, Malyshka, but we have to go. I need to see this through."

Her gaze hops from the pineapple she's poking at to my face. "And when it's over, will you kill my father?"

It would be easy to lie to her, tell her no, even though I plan to kill him soon. But I don't. "Not today. I won't kill him today."

We dress quickly, and I text Alexei to meet me at the car. He's been staying in another apartment so he's always nearby if we leave. I give him a nod as we climb into the vehicle to head to Arthur's compound. It kills me to take her back there, but she needs to see this end as much as I do. She just doesn't realize it.

It doesn't take long to get there, and I help her out of the back of the big SUV. She tugs down the hem of the sweater, then drops her chin to head inside.

I pull her back to me, my chest to her shoulder blades. "Lift your chin and stare straight ahead. You are my wife now, and you tuck tail for no one, especially a man who hurt you as incredibly as that one did."

She stiffens in my hold for a moment, then gently pulls from my grasp. But I'm proud to see she keeps her chin up and her eyes forward.

We wait by the door for Adrian and the others to arrive. The only other woman with us, besides Cilla, is Andrea. Of course, she'd want to be here most of all.

Her face is pale, even more than usual. She's pulled her long black hair back in a neat braid. I resist the urge to comfort her. That's not what we are to one another, and she'd shove me away regardless.

Alexei steps up behind his twin, following as she leads the way into the compound.

Arthur stands in a black three-piece suit at the end of the

hall. I recognize it to be the same one we escaped out of. The same one I'd been locked up in for several days.

I clench my fists, and Cilla pulls one toward her, uncurls my fingers, and laces hers along mine. I swallow, attempting to calm down. I have to be here for Andrea, for Valentina. This isn't just about me. There are others this family has hurt way worse. Sal may be dead, but everything he loved still stands, which is unacceptable.

Arthur leads us into a sitting room, but we all remain standing. "Can I offer you some refreshment, tea, coffee, whiskey?"

Adrian shakes his head and speaks for all of us. "This isn't a social visit. We are here to see to your end of the agreement and nothing more."

There's a slight slump to Arthur's shoulders as if he expected Adrian to walk in here as his friend. But he's Andrea's friend, Kai's friend, and as long as he is, he'll never be Arthur's.

Arthur walks to an intercom near the door and speaks into it. "Get them ready. We are coming down."

He leads us back down the hall to another room, this one sterile like a lab. When he opens a curtain, we spot bodies lined up neatly on the floor through the glass. They are awake and struggling. Every member of Sal's family runs his pedophile rings. Including the only man left who had a hand in Andrea's attack.

She steps up to the window. "Can they see us through here?"

Arthur nods, crossing his hands in front of him. "Yes, they can see you."

With a smile, she holds her hand up and flips the man off. All of them struggle against the rope bonds around their hands, their feet, and the gags in their mouths. I wonder what it took for him to do this to his own brother? Does he care? Somehow, I can't imagine he does, especially after what he did to his daughter over the years.

Adrian steps up beside Andrea and puts a supportive hand on the small of her back. He leans in and whispers too softly for anyone else to hear. When Andrea turns her face to speak to him, I spot tears shimmering in her eyes. She won't let them fall of course, but I'm glad she will finally be able to put this all behind her. Well, maybe once we get rid of Emmanuelle, she'll be able to.

Something doesn't sit right with me, though. I don't trust Arthur or his family, so I want to question everything. I stare at Arthur's solemn profile from across the room. "Why do this? How can you destroy your brother's family? Your family so easily?"

Arthur flicks his gaze my way, then locks back on the window. "Just because I'm not weeping doesn't mean I do this lightly."

"Then why?" Adrian asks, echoing my question.

There's more tension in Arthur's shoulders with all of us focused on him now. He might pretend to be indifferent, but he fears us enough to be wary. Good. "I'm tired of sitting on the outside while he runs our family name into the ground. His business was never going to be legitimate. He'll never be able to show his face in society without people like you sneering at him. He might not care about his image, but I care about mine. I care about our family legacy and won't have it tied any longer to peddling children's flesh."

Beside me, Cilla squeezes my hand, but she's not looking at Arthur. She's staring through the window as well. What does she see? Her uncle, or another man who would use her to break her?

Adrian focuses on Arthur, who, to his credit, doesn't flinch. "I believe some of that, but what else? You're not only doing this to resurrect your image."

Arthur waves at the window. "Maybe I want a seat at the

table. With this sort as my family, I'll never even get into the room."

I speak up again, unlocking my fingers from Cilla's and stepping forward. "Well, you aren't done with your end yet. After I kill them, you can call your side of the bargain complete."

Adrian cuts in front of me, his shoulder hitting my chest. "No. You won't kill them. This isn't just your revenge. We'll decide together who does it, and it'll be the person who will get the most from it."

All of our eyes, save Arthur's, stray to Andrea. She's not paying attention to any of us. Her eyes are still locked on that room, and I can't imagine what's happening in her head right now. Alexei steps up to stand beside her, his shoulder pressing into hers.

None of us speak as Alexei takes her hand in his, and she squeezes his back in response. She's going to be okay. Even after this revenge, it might take more time, but she'll be okay.

Adrian looks at Arthur again, his gaze cutting. "Is this all of them? You don't have any more cousins who might crawl out of the woodwork to come after one of mine again?"

Kai shifts beside me, his eyes focused on Arthur's answer. He can read people better than anyone. I know Adrian counts on him to read when people are lying.

Almost wringing his hands now, Arthur doesn't like to be cornered. "No. There is no one else. This is everyone who has a hand in the unsavory business or has been involved in plots against your family."

Adrian flicks his eyes to Kai, who gives a small nod. Barely perceptible if you aren't searching for it.

Arthur continues. "As for arguing over who will do the honors, there is no need. I've already administered a lethal dose of poison to each of them. They will breathe their last breaths in a matter of minutes."

The tension in the room ratchets as we all face Arthur as one. He holds his ground, no doubt knowing we wanted to be the ones to kill them. Adrian shifts a little closer. "What the fuck do you mean you've poisoned them."

"I mean, before you arrived, I gave them each a lethal dose of one of my drugs."

Andrea explodes forward, almost reaching him before her brother catches her around the waist. "So you what, give them something to make them feel good before they drift off to sleep peacefully? You fucking asshole. Do you know what they did to me? I'll kill you for this."

Arthur doesn't move, his eyes slipping between Andrea and Adrian. "The means of their death was never discussed. You told me to offer them up, and so I have. My extended family…" he pauses and glances through the window. "…is dead. Our business is concluded, and you all may go about your day and leave me to mourn my brother and his family."

Another squeeze on my hand makes me look down. Cilla stares out the window, the only one who keeps her gaze on them. "He was a bad man, as was his family. I had no love for them, but I can't believe he could just kill them all so easily."

I don't bother to pitch my voice low. "You don't believe the man who let his guards rape you as punishment could kill his own family? Really?"

Everyone's attention shifts to Cilla, except Arthur, who has turned to face the window now. But I know he's listening.

Andrea shoves out of her brother's arms and stalks to the door, leaving it to slam behind her. Adrian steps up to me and claps me on the shoulder. "There's nothing left here to do. I need to tell Val what happened."

Kai moves to the door leading into the other room. "Open it. I'm not stepping out of here until I feel all of their pulses. If they aren't dead, you're next."

Arthur presses a button, and I watch as Kai checks each already paling corpse. I can see the death on their faces. They're gone.

I step close enough to Arthur to be sure he can hear me. "I don't care what Adrian promised you. I don't give a shit if you think this makes us all even. I'll slit your throat and feel your blood run across my hands if it's the last thing I do."

Then we leave Arthur to his mourning and Kai to finish the details.

29

CILLA

I'm quiet through the rest of the night. Every so often, I feel his eyes on me, but I keep from making contact and only answer when necessary.

When I crawl into bed to stare out across the city, he enters the room behind me, shouldering the door into the wall with a percussive bang. "What the hell is your problem?"

I don't answer. It's not that I'm upset about the truly twisted side of my family. No one will miss those assholes. My father and how he could murder his own brother without even a glimpse of remorse has me shaken.

The bed shifts as he climbs and shuffles to my side. "Answer me when I ask you a question." His voice is a whip snap of annoyance.

I huddle under the covers further. "Don't worry about it. I'll be back to your sweet passive Cilla tomorrow. I'm not in the mood today."

I barely have the words out when his hand grasps my chin and yanks my head toward him. "What have I told you about that mouth?"

When I glare up at him, he tightens his grip. "You won't ignore me when I ask you a question."

Some of the fight leaves me with the firmness of his grip. Like I'm free to let some of my anger go to him. "I'm upset because my father is a monster."

One of his eyebrows raises. "You already knew that. Why be upset at the proof of it now?"

I sigh, rolling a bit to avoid pain in my neck at the angle. "It hurts me every time he does something heartless. I'm ashamed of him, of my family, and what that means for me. How long until I'm just as heartless?"

He settles on his ass and gentles his grip on my chin. "You could never be heartless, Malyshka."

"His blood is in my veins. He's a part of me. How could I not one day turn on those I love."

Again, he shifts to lie on his side along my body. "We aren't our parents. Their sins do not become ours."

I stare up at his face as he braces on his hand, looking down at me. "But some sins are too big, too horrible. Someone has to take the fallout."

He relaxes, so his head hits the pillow only inches from my face. "No. They don't. You don't have to take the blame for the horrible things he's done. You don't need to take the anger, pain, or any of the suffering he's caused on yourself. Not when you're one of his victims, the same as many others."

But that's not all that's bothering me. No. It's much worse than how horrible my father is. He sees through me in an instant.

"What else? What aren't you telling me?"

I swallow hard, the sound loud between us. "I..." I can't bring myself to say it, to get the words out when I don't want to know the answer.

"Don't make me pull it out of you." His voice is hard, but it doesn't scare me. It starts a slow warm tingle from my core up into my chest. My nipples go hard at the idea of him forcing me to tell him what I'm hiding, of him caring enough to make me reveal my secrets, bare myself to him completely.

As much as I want to see what he means, I swallow and shake my head. "It's just...I wonder how long I have until my name means my death, along with the rest of my family."

I thought he was angry when he walked in. But that was nothing compared to the black scowl that rolls across his face now.

He grabs my chin and tilts my face to a painful angle, forcing my eyes to follow him. "Now..." His voice is white-hot anger, so potent I can almost feel it in his hands. "The only way your name will get you killed is if someone is coming for me. You have MY name! You belong to ME! Not him. Say it."

I'm shaking now, even though I'm covered in the blanket. Not out of fear. My body is a live wire attuned to his anger, his needs, and his desires. All I feel is the urge to sate his anger, to throw myself at his feet and see what his mercy looks like when it marks my skin.

I gulp again. "I belong to you."

Even as I say it, some small part of my mind rebels at the thought. Why? Why do I always have to belong to someone else? I belonged to my father and now to Ivan. When do I get to belong to me?

"I can see you overthinking the question, Priscilla." He forces the words out in a snap. "If you want to push me tonight, I'll let you, and then you might regret it later."

If I know one thing, it's that I could never regret anything we do together. If he touches me angry, or horny, or in fear...never once has he given me something I didn't want, didn't need.

If this is what it means to belong to him, maybe it's not such a bad thing. My fucking heart is too stupid to shield itself. I've already known it belongs to him without question. Even if he doesn't want me in the same way.

Even though he says I have his name and protection, I can't imagine his friends feeling the same way. That his friends will be fine with a member of their enemy's family joining their own. They'd never accept me, and that's something I can't put him through. I can't put myself through watching him make the choice between them and me.

I don't doubt who he'd choose if he were forced to face the truth of our situation.

Something about what I'm feeling must show on my face because he rolls fast so I'm underneath him, and his hands are braced along my chest, holding his weight off the top of my body.

With him over me, staring down at my face, I take a minute to look at him. His face is etched with the battles he's fought, some scars, but most of all, the hard-as-steel look in his eyes.

Anyone else would likely find it terrifying, but I see the softness at the edges and the gentleness with which he twisted me under him. I hold myself still, waiting to see what he'll do next.

He holds his weight on one hand, his hips pressed between my thighs, and he uses the other hand to grapple with the zipper on my pants. The liquid sparks he's already started turn into a bright flare of molten lava through me.

I arch up into his grasp when his hand delves under my panties and cups around my pussy.

He slowly lowers himself to his elbow and puts his face in line with mine so his mouth rubs against mine as he speaks. "This cunt belongs to me. Say it."

I blink, trying to focus while his warm hand is on my most intimate flesh. "This cunt belongs to you."

Something predatory enters his eyes as he stares into mine. "Your body belongs to me."

His soft full lips caress mine in less than a kiss, more of a claim.

"My body belongs to you."

This time, he moves his fingers through my already-soaked center and spears me on two of them. "Your pleasure belongs to me."

I swallow, my body automatically tightening around the sweet invasion. "My pleasure belongs to you."

Still staring deep into my eyes, he snaps his teeth at my bottom lip, pulling it taunt and releasing it hard. "Your pain belongs to me."

I'm shivering now, needing so much more than these teases of sensation. "My pain belongs to you," I whimper.

He licks his lips, sending his tongue along mine as well. I arch up, trying to get more, but he doesn't allow it.

"Now, when you truly believe what you say, we won't have any more problems. For now, you'll take your punishment for all that attitude."

He lifts off me, kneeling between my thighs, and jerks my pants down my legs, my underwear half pulling with the fabric. I help him shove off the pants and drag my shirt and bra off to toss them away.

He stares down at me while he unbuttons his shirt. It's slow, teasing, as he reveals tattoos and scars to the glittering city lights sparkling through the windows.

It takes a little more effort to remove his pants. "Are you ready for your punishment? Tell me why I'm punishing you."

I swallow, knowing what he wants me to say, but the sheer adrenaline pumping through me makes it hard for me to speak.

"That's okay, Priscilla. You'll say it before I'm done with you."

He grabs my thighs and flips me onto my belly in one smooth move. The covers tangle around me, but I ignore them. When he pulls my hips up, sheer need grips me, and I press back into him. I'll beg him if he wants me to. I just need him inside me.

But he doesn't go for my pussy, his thumb skims my asshole, and I jerk forward in shock. I've had anal sex before, but it's never really been my thing.

Except now, when he thumbs the tight ring, my body lights up even more. I clench my thighs together, the emptiness there acute.

He grips me hard and leans down, and I feel warm liquid slide across the sensitive hole. It takes me a second to realize he's spit on me.

I barely have time to consider the next step when he's prodding my asshole with his cock, thick and seemingly so much bigger than ever before. Discomfort burns through me as he presses forward, and I whimper from the pain. I grit my teeth and brace my weight on my elbows, gripping the blankets while he stretches my ass enough to make room to move.

"I... It hurts. I don't think you'll fit." I whine, the feeling of being stretched beyond my limits ripples through me. I'm almost certain he will tear me in two at any moment.

"I'll make it fit." He groans, and I can feel the tears sliding down my cheeks. The rough edge of his words slices through me. True to his nature, he doesn't start slow to get me used to the feeling. He pounds into me so hard that, for a moment, the pain is all I feel. As if he knows this, he slips a hand beneath my body and rubs circles against my clit. Slowly the pain splinters into pleasure, and I bury my face in the blanket to cover the moans I can't seem to stop.

"This asshole belongs to me, Malyshka. Every inch of you," he grunts as he fucks into me harder. "Every fucking inch of you is mine to use, to own, and to protect."

Stars dance behind my eyes as he goes from rubbing circles

to pinching my clit, with one hand while he holds my hip in place with the other.

His cock stretches me even more as he seems to grow harder. The noises are obscene, and I can only think about the thin line between pain and pleasure. He gives my clit one more sharp pinch, and I splinter and completely fucking break apart for him.

"That's it, Cilla. My beautiful Cilla. Come for me."

He pounds me harder, my face shoving forward into the covers, pushing me up into the headboard. "You belong to me. This is all mine. All mine." His last words come out on the end of a grunt, and he comes, holding himself inside me, his hands gripping my hips hard, his pelvis fused to my ass.

When I'm finally aware of my senses, all I can hear is his heavy panting. Then... "Say it, love. Say it for me."

This time, I don't even think about it. "I belong to you. I belong to you." Tears track down my cheeks as the words give me a sense of comfort rather than fear for the first time in my life.

30

IVAN

Kai makes an all-call text early the next day. Part of me doesn't want to get out of bed with Cilla wrapped so sweetly and naked around the side of my body. I've never been much of a cuddler, but with her, it's different. Waking up beside her in the morning is as natural as breathing. I just want to take her in and keep her the longer I look at her.

But regret rises quickly. Not for touching or being with her, but because I'm an animal, and she doesn't deserve me. I'm one more punishment in a long line of painful punishments in her life.

She stirs when I climb out of bed. After dressing, I leave her a quick note telling her she can go to the casino later, as I'll meet her there. Once the meeting is done at the penthouse, I need to go there and ensure things are still on track.

I make it to the command room in the penthouse before almost everyone. Only Kai sits at his usual spot with the keyboards in front of him. The screens are going, and when I walk in, he clicks off and swivels to look at me.

I don't know how he can look like he walked out of a magazine photo shoot so early in the morning, but Adrian has the same uncanny ability.

I look like a junkie in stolen clothes this early. Especially before coffee. "What are you working on?"

Kai stands, stretches, and joins me by the coffee pot. "Just more research on chemists and drug manufacturers in the area. I set up some local alerts so that we get some information back if anyone posts something online."

Adrian walks in, followed by Alexei, Andrea, and Michail. Once we are all seated, Adrian reaches into the pocket of his charcoal gray suit and tosses a piece of paper on the table.

I don't even need to touch it to spot the council seal. "What the fuck do they want now?"

Adrian's jaw tightens. He seems to almost grind his teeth. "It's a punishment. A way for them to ensure I'm still in line. There's a vacuum where the bitch queen and Emmanuelle left. For now, we pretend we only want peace."

I stare around at my friends' equally stony faces. "Am I the only one thinking less like punishment, more like a trap. At the season closing party? Really?"

Kai shifts to look at Adrian. "A trap for the council, maybe? Is this our chance to take them all out?"

Adrian stares at the table, and we all wait while he thinks. A few minutes later, he gazes around the room again. "We aren't ready to take them all out yet. Soon. Very soon, but for now, we pretend we are team players."

I catch his eye. "Pretend what? That we are lap dogs that can be kicked around and never bite back? That's never been who we are."

Adrian's jaw tightens again. "Yes, true, but we have more to lose now."

Kai and Michail both shift uncomfortably. They agree, but they also have their wives to protect now. It hits me. I need to protect mine too. But that doesn't mean I want to roll over like a bitch for the council.

But this isn't my decision. Adrian is the one who makes the calls, and we follow. There might be another opportunity later to hunt the council one by one until they are all gone.

After the meeting, Alexei pulls Adrian to the side. I can't help but overhear. "What do we need to do for the party? Hosting here?"

Adrian leans in. "The order is that it is to be hosted here, and only here, to demonstrate our willingness to be a part of society."

I shake my head and walk out, intending to get to the casino before Cilla. A couple of the girls are in their usual spot at the bar, looking tired. It's early, but we like to provide entertainment at any time of the day.

The memory that Cilla used to be one of them hits me hard. I try to recall how many times I'd seen her go off with a client. It makes me want to break things, so I quickly shove the thoughts away.

I go to the office, get the schedules and books in order, and then return to the lounge floor.

It's quiet, with soft music playing, and that won't change until the afternoon when more patrons roll in.

When I wander near the bar, I spot Cilla standing a few feet away from the two prostitutes leaning on the polished wood.

I give them some space, watching them together. Cilla is smiling, wearing jeans and a red T-shirt. It only takes seconds to think about putting my mouth on her skin and her hands on my body.

"When are you coming back?" one of the girls asks. I can't remember her fucking name as we rotate the girls between the lounges, but her tone is short, and I don't appreciate that.

Cilla drops her chin, her shoulders dropping. "I'm not

coming back. I got married. I'm pretty sure he wouldn't appreciate my returning to work."

The anger rises fast enough that I have to clench my fists to keep from marching over there. But I both want to hear what the girls say to her and what she says to them.

The other girl eyes Cilla for a moment. "You sure seem different…"

Cilla's back stiffens. "I mean, you don't wear your hooker heels to the grocery store, do you?"

They giggle at each other and speak too softly for me to hear. I simply watch her as she interacts with her friends. The wave of longing hits me again, and I picture her asleep on my chest this morning. I rub at my sternum for a moment and push the thoughts away. As much as I want her, and as much as I need her, I'll never be worthy of her.

I focus on what they are saying again. Cilla takes a step back from the long-haired brunette to her left. I was distracted and didn't catch what she said to her…but Cilla's body language was enough to send me marching across the bar to her side.

The women retreat to the bar rail as I wrap my arm around Cilla's waist. "Ladies. Good morning."

The brunette recovers first, stepping up to my side. "Ivan. It's been a while since we've seen you. Come to play?"

Cilla slaps the woman's hand as it moves toward my suit jacket. "Don't touch him."

A smile curves across my face as I glance down at Cilla's fierce look. I tilt her chin up toward me. "Jealous, malyshka? That's kind of hot."

A pink wash hits her cheeks. "I just…I mean…"

The brunette pouts. "You don't get to keep every client you sleep with. If he chooses someone else, you have to step aside."

I keep Cilla's eyes on mine and dip my head to kiss her. She tastes like mint and coffee. I curve my hand to the back of her neck as I deepen the kiss enough that she grabs my arm, digging her nails into my jacket.

When I release her lips, she is dreamy-eyed, and her lips are swollen.

I speak again but to the brunette, keeping my eyes on Cilla. "I'm not her client. I'm her husband."

There's a soft gasp, and I realize Cilla made the sound. She clears her throat, and I've had enough of waiting to touch her. "Come with me."

I drag her back to the office by the forearm. Once inside, I lock the door, slamming her into the wood, and take her mouth again.

She clings to my shoulders, and when I trail my mouth down to her jaw, then her neck, she whimpers. "Is this all you wanted to do today? We could have stayed in bed for this. We didn't need to put on pants."

"You're right." I breathe against her skin. "Next time, no pants. I want you in a dress so I can touch this sweet little pussy anytime I feel like it."

I grab her pants, drop to my knees to rip them open, and shove her underwear to her ankles. The angle isn't ideal, but I bury my face into her sweet scent and lick up her body's seam.

God, even her taste calms me, sedating the demon inside. I suckle her clit and wrap my hands around the curve of her ass to cup the cheeks. Her fingers delve across my head until her nails dig into my bare scalp. I love the feeling of her pleasure marking me. "Spread your legs wider. Give me more of my pretty fucking pussy."

She shifts her stance, and I curve my hand to spear her as I drag my tongue from her opening to her clit, wetting her up even more. "You taste like heaven."

She moans and drops her head against the wood. But it's not

enough. "Louder, Malyshka. I want them to know how much I make you scream."

I spread her a little wider and push in a third finger. Her sheath tightens around me, silken and wet, as I lower my head to her clit again.

She rocks into my hand, into my face, as her knees shake around my ears. I lick her, my cock growing harder by the second. A rush of fluid makes me tug her clit between my lips so I can suck on the tiny nub hard enough to make her come for me. I want her release to coat my tongue. I want it dripping down my chin.

"More, Priscilla. All of it. Come for me, and I want you to scream my name as you do."

I quickly add a fourth finger and watch as she shudders and squeezes around my fingers. "That's it, baby, come."

I lap at her generously until she gasps my name, then screams it out into the empty room. The sound goes straight to my dick. The one I plan to fuck her face with later.

Gently, I ease my fingers from her core. "Shift your thighs so I can get up."

Her eyes glitter as she stares down at me. "What if I want you to stay there?"

"If I stay here, I'll never get any work done, and we'll spend the day naked on this cold floor."

She sighs, leaning into the door heavily. "Mmm...you're right."

I stand and adjust my hard dick. When she reaches for me, I stall her hands. "No, that was for you. This can wait until later. I plan to fuck you until you can't walk straight."

She gulps, and I'm satisfied by the hungry look in her eyes.

Once she is presentable again, I open the door and lead her to the bar. "You can stay here if you want, or I'll ask Alexei to take you home. I'll warn you now, we need to prepare for another party."

Her smile drops instantly. "Another party?"

"The season-ending party will be hosted by Adrian at the penthouse."

"Doesn't he usually use the hotel? I thought the penthouse was supposed to be protected."

I shake my head. "It is, but the council, and its new manager, after Emmanuelle's arrest, are worried about Doubeck taking over. They are worried Adrian will dismantle the useless council and society itself to take over everything."

Her eyes widen. "Is that what he plans to do?"

I kiss her again. "No one knows what Adrian plans to do until he decides. With Valentina super pregnant, he has no intention of putting her in danger. Kai and Michail feel the same way."

"And you?" she whispers.

I kiss her again, lead her to a booth, and then leave her with the question unanswered. I refuse to lie to her, and I don't think she wants to know how much I want her father dead.

31

CILLA

The next day, Ivan has to go back to work again. His worry over the upcoming party is palpable. My worries feel more trivial, considering what everyone else is facing. Without the threat of my father hanging over my head, my thoughts are consumed with Ivan. His non-answer about the fear of safety at the party has me worried and turned inside out.

Maybe after what I've done to him, what I dragged him into, he'll never be able to feel the same way for me as I feel for him. But I won't know unless I ask, and I'm too much of a chickenshit to ask him outright.

When he goes wherever he needs to go and doesn't see fit to enlighten me, I ask Alexei to take me to the penthouse. He sends a text off, which I assume is to ask permission, and then we head to the tower. Does he ask Adrian's permission or Ivan's? Why does one bother me, and the other doesn't?

Adrian greets me at the elevator, but I'm not here to see him. "May I talk to Valentina?"

The moment of hesitation puts another crack in my heart, but then I consider he might be this protective of her to anyone, not just me. If he's anything like Ivan, he's been doing nothing but hovering over Valentina's shoulder since the day she got pregnant.

When Adrian doesn't answer, I stare around the foyer. It's a lovely penthouse. It would need to be for all of them to live here together and not go insane.

Valentina walks slowly into the room, holding under her very rounded belly, her hair curly and wild around her shoulders. "Cilla, come on in. Ignore him. He's freaking out because of the pregnancy. Come on, let's go sit in the library and have some coffee."

Adrian clears his throat. But she simply blows him a kiss. "She can have coffee while I try to smell her cup. I'll have decaf tea."

Fuck, they are adorable together. I get another pang in my chest. Ivan and I will never be this way.

I follow her into the library, feeling self-conscious in the lavender sweater and jeans I wear. She's wearing something similar with leggings instead of jeans. Still, I always feel super underdressed around all these men and their suits. Not to mention, the suit reminds me of previous clients. A part of my life I don't want to remember. I'm not against sex work, but forced sex work is exploitation. Now that I'm out of the situation, I can see what my father was doing was exploitation.

We sit on cozy chairs in the library, and I close my eyes for a second to breathe in the scent of books. "This is lovely. I'm not a very fast reader, but I love them. The smell is one of my favorite parts."

Valentina settles back on a pillow and props her feet up on the coffee table. "I love this room. I'd love it more now if this tiny person would get the fuck out of me, and I could sit comfortably on any furniture in the penthouse. You should see my bed; we are swimming in pillows I use to keep things propped and padded."

I stare at her belly for a moment. "How are things going with that? The doctor says things will be all right? When are you due?"

"Not for another month, but I feel like I'm as big as a house, so I want it to be now. I'd super love to see my feet again and be able to bend over. My only consolation is that Adrian finds my pregnant state super sexy, which means…" She blushes. "Well, I'm sure you can imagine."

I shift on the seat. Just as I'm about to ask her what I came to ask, the door opens, and a small man brings a tray with tea and coffee.

Val shifts over but then sinks back into the chair. "Thank you, Max. We've got it from here."

The man—Max—nods once and leaves, closing the door behind him. I wonder what it's like to have a servant to wait on your every need.

Instead of dwelling, I pour a cup of tea for her, and she balances it on her belly.

With my coffee on my lap, I swallow hard and stare at my feet. "What do you know about Ivan?"

Val studies me. "Why do you ask?"

Another wave of worry hits. Of course, she'd be suspicious. She doesn't know me or my motivations. So maybe it will help to lay my cards on the table. "I love him. I'm ridiculously in love with him. But he's not letting me in. When I think we've made progress, it's like the next day, we go backward."

Val snorts. "That's not an Ivan thing. That's a man who grew up in this twisted society thing. All these men are emotionally unavailable."

I wave at the door. "You seem to have done all right."

"My relationship started the same as everyone else's…me

running for my life, and Adrian deciding he wanted me instead. That's how these guys seem to operate."

I smile. "What about Andrea?"

She shrugs and sips her tea gingerly. "I wouldn't be surprised if she's the same. She'd probably pick a guy, knock him out, and drag him back to her bed. I suspect he won't mind when he wakes up, but still."

Chuckling into my coffee, I relax for the first time since I arrived. "Anything that can help?"

Val shifts uncomfortably. "I mean... of the five, he is probably the one person I know the least about. He keeps to himself. He gets angry a lot but still seems to be able to control himself, which makes him better than most of the men I've met in my life."

"Mine too," I murmur.

After that, we sit in silence for a moment, drinking. I grab a small shortbread cookie off the tray. Of course, it's perfect.

I'm lost in thought when Val speaks again. "What are you going to do?"

Blinking, I shake my head. "I suppose I have to tell him. I don't think he will care, or he might try to push me away sooner. I honestly have no idea."

"You should tell him. He deserves to know. Even if he doesn't feel the same way, you will at least know the truth and can stop obsessing over it. Although, if I'm being honest, I've never seen him look so happy as the day you married. There was some kind of peace etched into his features that I'd never seen before. I think he cares for you and shows it in other ways that aren't words."

I nod, squaring my shoulders. "You're right. I should just tell him. Get it out of the way, and stop stressing about it."

She raises her teacup to me. "To love."

I don't toast to that. So far, love is the worst. "I'll tell him," I repeat to myself.

"Tell me what?" Ivan's deep voice rumbles through me like a slow rockslide. Fucking hell.

I place my cup on the table. "Nothing, we are just having some girl talk."

Val lumbers upward. "Right. Periods, pads, girl things."

He narrows his eyes at her. "Unlike the pussies you seem to have met before, I have no fear of your biological functions."

Val chuckles and then groans. "I'll leave you two kids alone. It's past my nap time. Adrian will hunt me down soon if I'm not in bed resting."

Ivan holds the door open for me. "Let's go home. I can do the rest of the work I need to take care of while we are there."

I stand and give Val a smile. "Thank you for spending time with me."

She sighs. "I might just nap right here. See you guys later."

It doesn't take long to get back to the apartment. Once inside, he strips his jacket off and tosses it over a chair. "What did you want to tell me?"

I shake my head. "Nothing, really. We were just chatting about things. Want me to cook something? I'd love to do that for you."

He cups my hips and dips his lips to my neck. "How often have I told you that you don't have to do that? I can order something from probably anywhere and get it here in record time. I just want to touch you right now."

He backs me into the bedroom until I hit the bed and fall backward. I shift until he can join me.

When he doesn't go for my clothes, I freeze. "What's happening here?"

He tugs me into the curve of his body, both of us fully dressed. "I just want to hold you right now. Feel you against me."

The slow drum of my heartbeat in my body calms, and a new kind of warmth spreads. Fuck, I'm so gone over him. It's going to kill me when I lose him.

"Stop thinking" His voice is a deep rumble in my ear. "I can feel the tension in your back. This is supposed to be relaxing."

The hard bar of his cock against my ass singes my nerve endings. "Are you relaxed that way?"

He rocks his hips against me. "Very fucking relaxed, Malyshka. As much as I want you, we don't have to always be fucking when I touch you."

His statement has a soft undertone, and I latch on to it. I roll and pull his head onto my chest to run my fingers over the stubble on his scalp. What does his hair look like when he grows it out? He's always kept his head cleared, his tattoos on full and intimidating display.

He rumbles and breathes heavily against me. "That feels nice."

We lie there for hours, the sun disappearing and the city lights flickering in the window. Neither of us moved. At some point, I fell in and out of sleep, as did he. I don't know what time it was, but at some point, I felt him shift his thigh over mine and cuddle closer to me, clutching me to him with an intensity I could barely breathe through.

The only thing I could do is clutch him back and hold him tight. I told myself I'd tell him, and right now, I feel it more than ever. So I take a deep breath and whisper it to the night. "I love you."

He obviously doesn't respond, no doubt passed out, but a tiny glimmer of hope wishes he would. I lie in silence, listening to him breathe, and eventually, let my eyes close and night take me under.

32

IVAN

Every day I spend with her, I think more and more that I can't be worthy of someone like her until I kill her father. Until I destroy the man who hurt her so badly. It won't be enough until I can feel his blood on my skin and know he will never hurt her again.

She seems to care less about her father or what he means to how our life is going. But Arthur is hanging over my head, reminding me every day that there's still someone out there who can threaten her.

It's late morning when I find her in the closet studying her clothes. "How did I get so many things so quickly? I'm used to being able to pack everything in a duffel bag."

I lean on the door and watch her, not interested in the clothing unless I'm peeling them off her. "The party is coming up quickly. You'll get another dress to wear."

She sighs and slides her hands down the sleeve of a blouse. "Do I really need another one? I have a few in here already."

As much as she complains, I notice her caressing the silk and cashmere in the closet. "We have to present a united front. We'll all be dressed in similar colors."

With a smile, she turns. "Like a knight in a fairy tale wearing their lord's colors?"

"If that's how you want to think about it, sure."

She studies me and no doubt sees something in my face that I don't bother trying to hide from her. "Let me guess, we are wearing a whole shit ton of black."

I chuckle, and she freezes. "Did you just...laugh?"

Now I narrow my eyes at her. "Don't overthink it. Anyway, this party is the last one of the season, so once it's over, we'll have at least a few months of freedom before the season opens again. It'll give us time to plan how to get out of the council's crosshairs and keep our family safe."

"I thought Michail's wife was on the council. Can't she help?"

"She's on the Chicago council and was in touch with Emmanuelle, who turned out to be an FBI agent and was removed from his council position. So that whole thing is pretty complicated."

This is the most I've discussed our family business with her, and I can't tell if she wants to know more or wishes she knew less.

A moment of silence, and then she nods toward the closet. "So what do I need to do right now to help us get ready?"

I grab her belt loops and pull her into my body. "Right now, we must go shopping for something very important."

"What?"

I bite her neck gently, loving the look of my mark on her pale flesh. "You'll see when we get there."

She doesn't need much convincing to get into the car. Once again, Alexei drives us, staying nearby as we head into the small jewelry shop we have all taken to shopping at. The owner isn't in, but the manager, who recognizes all the Doubecks, immediately locks the doors and is ready for whatever we need.

I wave at the brightly lit display cases. "We need jewelry for the event. Pick what you like."

She freezes and hugs her middle. "This isn't necessary. I don't need anything."

I close the tiny bit of distance between us and lift her chin. "I will only say this one time. You, like me, represent our family when we go to events like this. That means you need to look the part, act the part, and do anything to protect our interests."

She gulps, and I cup the back of her neck and lean down to kiss her. "Now pick out whatever you like so I can take you home, strip you naked, and see what your skin looks like when it's covered in jewels."

When she sways into me, her eyes drifting closed, I know I've got her.

She finally steps up to the cases and looks around. "Was I right? Are we wearing black?"

I align my hips with her ass and stare over her head. "Yes, the clothes are black. So pick something that will match."

She points at the smallest diamond studs in the case, and I sigh.

"If you make me choose for you, I will buy the most expensive item in this store."

She leans down to the case again, and her eyes catch on fire-red stones set in platinum with diamonds around the outside. But she doesn't ask to see them.

I reach around her and point at the earring and matching necklace set. "Can we see this one, please?"

The saleswoman lays the pieces out on a plush velvet cloth. "These are one-of-a-kind pieces and can complement any ensemble."

Ignoring Cilla's gasp when she sees the price tag, I scan the case again. "Do you have bracelets to match?"

She rushes to another case and brings back two matching garnet bracelets. Now, I focus on Cilla. "How do you like these?"

I give her a few seconds to process. She moves to another case, out of my grasp. "What about this one?"

I lean over to stare at a thick, brilliant gold arm cuff. It's intricately carved and beautiful. "If that's something you like, it's yours."

The manager rushes to grab it and then waits for more instructions.

I let her take her time and enjoy watching her eyes zero in on the smaller items, then shift to what she really likes almost involuntarily. Each time I motion to the woman and have her pull out the pieces.

Cilla gasps at the array of jewels on the velvet when she returns to the main case. "I don't need all of this. Just give me a moment to figure out which I want to take with us."

My patience with shopping is done, so I shake my head and turn Cilla to face me. "We are going home. They will deliver the pieces later."

With that, I nod and circle my finger to indicate the saleswoman can wrap it all up. "Please put it on my account."

She stumbles over her response as we turn to the door. "Yes, of course. We'll wrap them up and send it all today. Thank you, sir."

We head back to the apartment, and Cilla still looks a little shocked.

I lead her to the bedroom and sit her on the bed. "Malyshka, do you remember what I said about arguing with me in public?"

She jerks, her eyes dropping to where I'm stripping off her shoes. "What? That wasn't arguing."

"I told you to pick, and you didn't listen every single time. So now, I get to reinforce the message."

She grabs my shoulders. "What are you going to do?" Her voice is husky and breathless.

It grabs me by the balls and makes me want to lay her back and open her up like a feast.

"Right now, I'm going to take your clothes off. Then while you're beautiful and naked, I'm going to put you on your knees so I can fuck that gorgeous mouth until you can't argue with me anymore."

She shudders as I pull her to her feet and strip the rest of her clothes off. When she's naked, she sinks down to the floor and grabs for my zipper. She's almost frantic as she rips down the zipper and pulls out my already achingly hard dick.

Her tongue rakes over my swollen head, and then she suck me in deep. Fucking hell, she is good at this. I can't bear to think about how, so I enjoy the moment, forcing all thoughts away.

I give her a moment to set her own pace, enjoying how she moans with every swipe of her tongue. "Keep going, baby. Your mouth feels so good on me."

She doesn't even move off me to respond. Her sole focus is on my dick and how she grips me at the base and swirls her tongue back to the head over and over.

When I start to get close to coming, I pull her head off me by the hair at the base of her neck. "Stop, baby. It's time for your punishment. What kind of lesson will you learn if you love every second of this?"

She narrows her eyes. "Who says I love it?"

I kneel in a second and grab her bare cunt. My fingers slide almost inside her with how soaked she is. "I think your body betrays you."

With a smile, she nips my bottom lip. "Okay, fine. I love making you feel good. It turns me on more than anything else."

"Well, then, I guess I should use you a little harder than normal so you learn your lesson this time."

She swallows hard, a shiver rolling through her.

I stand and tug her by the hair back to my cock. "Now, suck it, and don't stop until I come down that pretty throat."

She sucks me deep and then wraps her hand back to my ass, digging her nails into my ass-covered pants. I regret leaving my clothing on, wanting to feel her sharp little claws draw blood as I choke her with my dick.

I grab the back of her head, my palm flat on the crown, and start using her mouth hard. She relaxes, taking everything I have to give. Her mouth doesn't feel as amazing as her pussy, but the way her body leans into me is impressive. It's like she is using her entire body to suck me off.

She drags her teeth in one of the passes, adding the tiniest hint of pain to the motion. It shoots straight through me, bringing me to the edge of my orgasm in a few tiny movements.

"Not a chance, Malyshka. This isn't going to be over that fast. Open wider." I jam my dick straight to the back of her throat. She gags, and it only makes me harder. When she moans, I truly understand how much she loves this. How much she needs it. Finally, something I feel qualified to give her. Something I can offer for the gift of what she gives me so selflessly.

I fuck her good and hard, and soon, she's completely relaxed. The head of my cock brushes the back of her throat, and my orgasm rises quickly. "Get ready for it. I'm going to shoot my load down your throat, and I want you to swallow every drop. If even one escapes, I'll make you do it again until you can do it right."

She hums in the back of her throat, and I come so hard I see stars behind my eyelids. Holy fucking shit.

She continues sucking even as I stall in the wake of my orgasm. When I stop completely, she pulls away and stares up at me with watery eyes and swollen lips. Not a single drop of my cum escaped her mouth.

I kneel, my pants tight over my knees, and I wipe the corner of her mouth. "That was so fucking sexy. You are amazing."

She clears her throat. "I loved that. So much." Her voice is deep and scratchy.

I carry her to bed and make warm tea to soothe her raw throat.

When she passes out in my arms, I stare at the ceiling and circle back to what's been on my mind all day. I'll never be worthy of this gift until I get rid of Arthur.

33

CILLA

I watch the clock on the day of the party, and it seems to fly. No matter how much closer we get to the time I need to start preparing, the boulder in my gut hasn't shifted.

If Ivan notices my unease, he doesn't say anything. I'm probably being ridiculous, but I have a bad feeling about the party and what it means to be under the council's thumb.

Being an invisible part of my father's life, I never had to deal with council activities. Now it seems I'll be front and center for all the events.

When the alarm goes off, indicating I need to start working on my hair, I feel like I might be sick. This gets Ivan's attention while he starts his own preparations. "What's wrong?"

I hold my curling iron and stare at him in the mirror. "I don't know. I just have a bad feeling. Can't we stay home tonight? Doesn't Adrian have all the protection he needs already in place?"

"Don't ask me not to be there for him. I can't do that. When he walks into the fire, I will be at his side."

The boulder shifts and grows. "But you drag me in as well. Doesn't that mean anything to you?"

I finish the curl and set the hot iron on the bathroom counter. "I just worry about what's going to happen tonight. How will we know if something is up?"

Ivan pulls me close to stare down the line of my body, studying my black lingerie. "I pretty much assume there is always something up. That way, I'm already prepared."

I turn in his arms and press my chest to his bare one. "What if we stay here, and you punish me for making us miss the event?"

He tilts my chin and wraps his hand around the back of my neck, and I love when he does it. When his fingers close around half my neck, it makes me feel so cherished and owned—but in a way that makes me feel special, not pathetic.

"We have to go, Priscilla. I won't hear anything else about staying home."

I reach for his still-open zipper. "Are you sure?"

He snaps his hand around my wrist and pulls my hand away. "If you keep it up, I'll save your punishment until we get home. So don't keep pushing me."

I sigh and face the mirror again, returning to curling my hair. I didn't think my teasing would convince him, but I had to try. Especially when leaving for this party is making me want to puke.

He watches me in the mirror, but I keep my eyes on my hair, trying to hide the tears building in my eyes. I know this is a bad idea. I feel it in my gut, but I don't have a way to convince him, and he obviously doesn't love or trust me enough to believe me when I try to explain.

A few minutes into curling my long hair, he is mostly dressed and staring at me from the doorway. "Why are you so upset, Malyshka? Tell me."

I shake my head and focus on gathering my curls into an elaborate twist at the nape of my neck. "I just have a bad feeling. I can't explain it. My stomach is twisted in knots, and I think I'm just being ridiculous. I've never been to a society event, but I've heard horror stories about complete slaughters that can occur there."

He takes the pins from the counter and gently slides them in the places I indicate. "The slaughter mostly happens at the beginning of the season, not the end. Most are tired of the bloodshed by the closing party and want to get back to peace."

"Do you know who is going to be there? Should I be worried I might see a former client?"

His fingers tighten against my hair, then relax. "If you do, and they make you feel disrespected in any way, please let me know."

I roll my eyes even though he's not looking at my face. "Why? So you can kill them immediately."

"Why not? This is my last chance to get it out of my system. I'll fucking chop him in pieces in the middle of the dance floor, and the entire assembly will simply shift around the growing puddle of blood."

I pull his hands down to look at him. "Didn't you say the slaughter is at the beginning?"

He bends down, kissing me gently. Then spins me toward the bedroom. "There are always exceptions. People give me a wide berth. If someone sees me with you, they will do the same for you. At least if they have any sense."

I dress with his help and occasional groping as he enjoys the different textures over my skin.

Once we are ready to leave, he loads himself up with weapons and slides a knife into my clutch. "Just in case."

I don't argue, and we head to the penthouse. Everyone is already there when we arrive. Andrea and Alexei look every inch the twins they are, wearing the same color. My dress is black velvet and hugs every inch of my body. Andrea is wearing silk, and Valentina, with her rounded belly, is dressed head to toe in sparkling knit. Even as pregnant as she is, she looks incredible and so much more poised than me.

Even though my dress is beautiful, I feel like I don't belong. Kai's wife, Rose, is wearing a suit like the men, but her curves make it even sexier than they look.

Adrian steps to the center of the foyer, where we've all congregated. "This is going to be a fucking mess. Keep your eyes open and watch each other's backs. If something goes wrong, the women get Val out through the pre-planned route as fast as possible."

Since they didn't share this route with me, I assume I'm not part of the escort committee.

We all head down the elevator to another floor, where Adrian has the party set up. Society members are already milling around, drinking, talking, and laughing. It's a grating soundtrack to the worry in my belly.

Valentina grabs my arm, and Adrian follows at our backs while she tugs me to the bar. "Get this woman a whiskey."

Adrian gives her a look I can't decipher, and she shakes her head. "I'm going to smell it, that's all, I promise."

The bartender hands me a whiskey on the rocks, and I let her sniff it before I take a long draw. It soothes the ache inside me a tiny bit. But I don't trust the situation enough to lean into it for comfort.

I scan the floor for Ivan, but he's already disappeared in the rapidly growing crowd. Everyone is dressed incredibly, jewels winking at their throats and ears under the romantic lighting.

"Why do you look so pale?" Val asks, her eyes scanning the people around us.

I take another drink. "I'm not sure. I just have a bad feeling. If my father is coming, that's reason enough to feel shitty about being here tonight. Ivan made it clear staying home wasn't an option."

Val's eyes rake over me, and she focuses on the crowd. "Yes, they like to get their own way, don't they?"

Adrian leans down and nips her neck. "I heard that, angel. Keep it up."

With Adrian so close, I do feel a bit better. People seem to give him a wide circle of space, not wanting to risk offending or even jostling him. Andrea and Alexei cut through the room like beautiful pillars. People instantly seem drawn to them both. I can't blame the partygoers. They are both stunning.

When I spot Ivan, I squeeze Val's hand, then head over to his side. "See anything interesting yet?"

His jaw is tight, and his eyes are splinters of darkness. He's one step away from tossing people around the room. I curl my hand around his forearm and then slide my hand down to intertwine our fingers. "Everyone seems normal and like they are having a good time."

Ivan tilts his head toward a man across the room. "That's the fucker who insisted we use our home for this fucking shit show. I am debating if I want to see what his brains look like with the decor."

I turn to cut in front of him, forcing him to look at me. "Well, it won't match this outfit, that's for sure. Or yours, for that matter. We'll scare everyone out the door if you go and start killing people before they even bring out the hors d'oeuvres."

The corner of his mouth ticks as he stares into my eyes. "Maybe you're right. If he steps out of line, I'll end him. For now, he can enjoy his champagne."

I tug him close. "Do you want to dance?"

"I don't care to dance right now."

When he keeps his eyes on me, I give him a little pout, letting my red lips pucker, drawing his attention. "Please. Let's relax a little bit. Dance with me."

He scans the crowd, making sure the others are near Adrian and Val, then pulls me to the dance floor.

Thankfully, the song is slow, and I get to feel his hands slide around my waist to pull me tight to his body. "Have I told you how amazing you look tonight?" he whispers.

"You look beautiful too." I smile.

We spend time staring at each other. The room seems to shrink around us, putting us in our own little bubble. I can't help but wonder, and the words fall out of my mouth before I can reconsider. "Why did you marry me?"

My heart is pounding, and I'm so terrified to hear the answer that all I can hear is the whoosh whoosh whoosh of my own heartbeat in my ears.

It's a question I've been dying to know the answer to, and I've been too scared to come out and ask him. Why the fuck I think this is the best time, I don't know.

"Why did you marry me?" he counters.

I scoff. "Maybe because you didn't give me a fucking choice."

His eyes go from laughing to solemn in a second. "You didn't give me a choice either."

His words sink in, and I can't bring myself to hope he means what I want him to mean.

I open my mouth to ask him to elaborate when I spot a familiar face across the room.

My tense posture must have put Ivan on edge because he stops in the middle of the floor to stare at the way he caught me looking.

My father strolls in alone, his eyes scanning the crowd and locking on Ivan, then me. When he sneers, Ivan starts forward, but I throw myself in his path. "Not now, okay? You said slaughter is at the beginning. Let me enjoy my first society party without bloodshed."

He catches my hips and clenches tight into my dress. I stay still, staring up at him. When he drops his face to my neck, breathing deep, I relax, knowing he's not going to murder my father right this second, at least.

After a minute of standing on the floor, his face in my neck, everyone moving around us, he lifts his head. "Let's get a drink. It'll help get me through this night."

It only takes a minute to find the bar and another to get our drinks. We face the room, and I catch the smug look on my father's face as he stares at us, standing hand in hand from across the room. If he wants to survive the night, he better stay out of Ivan's way. I don't think alcohol is going to help with his temper.

Adrian cuts over in front of us. "How's it going?"

I sigh. "Well, Ivan hasn't killed anyone yet, so I call that a win."

Adrian makes a low noise in his throat. "Pity. This party could use some entertainment."

34

IVAN

I'm crawling out of my skin. Val and Adrian here in this pit of vipers make me want to slaughter anyone who even glances our way. Alexei and Andrea work the crowd, playing the society darlings they usually do. Kai flanks Val and Adrian like he's ready to jump at a moment's notice. Michail is away in Chicago, and I'm distracted.

Both Cilla being so close to me, and her father circling the same room, like a shark that smells blood in the water, is enough to keep my attention split. Not to mention, I fucking hate these events.

At least the crowd seems content. No bloodshed yet. I told Cilla the slaughter happens at the beginning of the season. Still, there is usually at least an attempt before the ending party concludes.

I hope it's Arthur, but as long as it's not me and mine, I don't give a shit.

Even as I clutch Cilla to my side, I keep my eyes on Arthur's back. He's chatting with some of the crowd, working his way through the party members, turning up the charm with the laughter coming from his circles.

Every time the man turns, he glances our way, his eyes straying over our party like he's waiting for something. I don't trust it one bit.

I can feel the time slipping through my fingers. When the clock strikes midnight, the party ends, and the bloodshed along with it. Any action after the chimes will result in a declaration of war. Not something I'm willing to risk with Adrian's child on the way.

I leave Cilla with Adrian and Val. The distance might give me some clarity. I keep my eyes on Arthur as I approach Andrea and pull her toward me.

At first, she snarls at me but follows me when she sees my face and that I'm not some stranger taking hold of her.

I lead her out to the floor and turn her in my arms to face me. "Try not to look so tense."

She flips her hair with a jerk of her neck. "I'm tense because you're touching me, and I don't know why. What the fuck are we doing?"

I keep my eyes on Arthur as we move around the room. "You're dancing with me. I'm trying to figure out how to slit Arthur's throat before the clock hits midnight."

She snorts, relaxing slightly. "Cutting it a bit close, aren't you?"

When I don't chuckle at her joke, she rolls her eyes. "Well, you don't have much time this evening. And you should probably wait until your new wife isn't looking so she doesn't get covered in her own father's blood."

"I don't think she will actually care after what he put her through."

She makes a noise and focuses off, letting me lead. "Well,

Adrian might, considering we are all supposed to be on our best behavior."

"I think he'll get over a little disobedience, considering what Arthur has put us through and what he's a party to currently. He can only cause us further grief with the more power he amasses."

Some of the other society members mill close to where we dance, thinking they might cut in. I make eye contact with each of them, daring them to try. "Where's your brother?"

She shrugs, grinning at the unease of the men circling, waiting for their opening with her. "He's off getting himself into trouble, no doubt. You know how the wives like to fawn over him, try to get him into their beds. It's a game to them, even though none of them ever succeed. The same thing they tried with Michail. Although, less so now with his wife's council position."

We stay silent for a moment, each of us keeping our eyes on our respective targets. Every so often, I trail my gaze to Cilla. She's stayed with Adrian and Val. Thankfully, she's smart and knows where she'll be safest. Only one of the things I adore about her.

I'm dying to say the words she wants to hear, but I can't bring myself to utter them while her father lives.

"What's your plan?" Andrea's voice cuts my attention.

"Slit his throat open and watch him bleed out on this gleaming floor."

She takes a deep breath and forces it out of her nose. "Typical. You are thinking about the results, not how you can get there without issue."

I spin us so I can focus properly on Arthur again. "I don't need a plan when the bastard stands six feet from us."

The sound of metal on crystal cuts the music, leaving the

ballroom filled with loud voices. The dancers stop, and I shift both of us so no one stands at our backs.

Adrian steps in front of the crowd, looking every bit the dark king he is. No one can look away from him when he wants attention.

Val steps up to his side and wraps his arm around her back. "Thank you for joining us for the closing of the season. There have been a lot of changes this year." He makes eye contact with Ripley, the new council head. "And I expect there are more changes to follow. But we'll endure, as we always do."

He raises his glass, and a few people join him. Some watch the others around them, and all of us who came with Adrian keep watch over who sneers and refuses to clap for his speech. A bold move in his own home.

Andrea's attention is elsewhere, and I slip behind her to move up behind Arthur. To put myself within reach of him at least. If he notices me and worries, all the better.

But he doesn't seem to be aware of his surroundings at all. Either he's got balls the size of a fucking watermelon, or he's an idiot. I'm leaning toward being an idiot.

The crowd mills around as the music restarts. I feel a little guilty leaving Andrea to her pit of vipers, but I know she can handle them.

My window of time is closing rapidly. Cilla will forgive me for abandoning her, and Adrian will forgive me for disobeying his orders. And even so, I'm willing to pay whatever price necessary once Arthur is dead.

I keep circling through the crowd. Whenever someone notices me close to them, they automatically shift away. A tactic I don't mind one bit. Considering my reputation, I don't blame them either. Too bad Arthur didn't take what they said about me seriously.

Alexei shifts by a couple of people to join me. "Whatcha doing?"

I roll my eyes at him and shake my head. "What the fuck does it look like?"

He shrugs and bumps my shoulder. "Like you're a lion in the wild stalking your prey."

"What do you want?"

Another shrug and a smirk to go along with it. Lucky me.

"My sister sent me over to make sure you don't get yourself killed by doing something stupid with no one at your back."

I scan the crowd, locking my eyes on Adrian again. He's fine with Kai, Val, and Cilla still standing with him. Everyone else gives them distance. As long as people keep doing that, we'll all make it out of here alive.

"Are you going for the old man? Anything I can do to help?"

I don't let him distract me and keep my eyes locked on Arthur's back. "No. You can't help. This is mine and no one else's. Understand?"

"You don't need to freak out on me. I'll make sure you get to cut his fucking head off if that's what you want. I don't give a shit. There is only one bastard still on my hit list, and I imagine I'll get to strike that name very soon."

This catches my interest. Alexei is the least damaged of all of us. With Sal's family gone, who could he possibly have in his sights? "Who?"

Alexei makes one of those stupid sarcastic, I don't know faces at me. I only glare back. "Stop fucking with me. Who are you going to kill? Are you waiting for the season to open or…"

His grin turns into a full toothy smile. "Oh, I don't need to. He's an FBI agent in jail. I'm sure the system will take care of itself in that regard. I don't need to lift a finger. But I might reward someone if I can find out who did the actual deed."

Has he noticed the charged looks between Emmanuelle and

his sister? Or is this about his sister's attack and Emmanuelle's role in it? Either way, in my mind, he's justified in wanting the man dead. I couldn't care less either way. Not when I have my own interests and targets. Speaking of targets...I hunt through the crowd and find Arthur again. He's shifted to near a wall. The perfect place to sneak up behind him and take care of business.

Alexei slinks with me, then cuts off to the side as I shift along the wall to set up behind Arthur. He notices me immediately but doesn't look the least bit scared. "Ivan. I wondered if you would come to me tonight. You're cutting it short on time, aren't you?"

"And you seem rather calm for a man about to have my blade inside him. And not in a kinky way." I study him. He does seem unnaturally calm, considering the situation. It should worry me, but I'm too focused on the fact that I'm finally going to get what I've been craving.

"You can make your move but know that if you manage to kill me, you're going to get your dearest friend killed."

My eyes shift to Adrian, who appears perfectly content talking to Cilla near the bar. Val and Kai are at the other end of the room. Of course, he'd have Kai go with her. For the first time in my life, I understand what it means to have my heart vulnerable outside my chest. If something happens to me, it doesn't matter. If something happens to her, well, I can't survive that the same way.

"He looks fine to me. Maybe don't worry about my friends and worry about yourself?"

Arthur steps closer, giving me the opening I've been waiting for. All I see is him, and he blocks out my view, or thought, of anyone else. It's not how I planned, but I sink my blade right into his gut. With such a sharp knife, it takes nothing to twist and shove it farther into his frail body. "You see, unlike you, I don't need to focus on anything but my prey. You do know what they call me, don't you?" I lean in and whisper, pulling him close and pushing the knife deeper. "The animal. The maniac. The killer. All the things they've said about me over the years. And you thought you could beat me at my own game?"

A dribble of blood spills over Arthur's thin lips, and for the first time in a while, I smile and watch. He coughs once, then chuckles, a loud raspy liquid sound now that his lungs are filling with blood. "You might have killed me, but like I said, you also killed your friend."

I shift my gaze one more time, taking my eyes off the dying man, to seek out Adrian.

But he's no longer where I left him. The sounds in the room start to register through my pounding heart and adrenaline.

Time skips.

I release Arthur to fall to the floor, blood staining his clothes and my hands.

People scatter out of the way, leaving me a trail right to Adrian. He's down, but then I see Cilla, flat on her back on the floor, a stain spreading over her skin the same color as Arthur's.

Val is gone. Kai is gone. Andrea is gone. All escaped through the rapidly dwindling crowd.

Alexei stands a few feet away, restraining a woman around the neck, a gun pressed into the side of her body.

I drop to my knees, sliding to reach them. "What..."

Cilla's eyes are closed, and she's pale.

Adrian is holding her stomach closed with his hands. "She saved my life. This woman made her move, and Cilla pushed me out of the way, taking a bullet."

His voice reaches me, but all I can see is her. "Come back, Priscilla. Don't you dare leave me when I haven't told you what I need to say. Come back to me."

35

CILLA

All I can hear is him whispering over and over to come back to him. It's in my head, reverberating like a gong. If gongs are sexy as hell and turn me inside out.

The night comes back in snatches. Adrian shouting. Val murmuring softly. Ivan whispering over and over to me as I lie flat on my back. The cold marble beneath me.

There was music and dancing, Ivan looking so good in his tuxedo. I spent time talking to Adrian and enjoyed seeing his softer side as he gazed after his wife standing with Kai.

I don't know what drew my attention. The quick move she made or the way her hand flew up unnaturally. I reacted out of sheer instinct. One my father beat in to me over the years. If he hadn't beaten me or let others beat me, I might not have developed such a keen sense of perception to remain as safe as I could.

I blink my eyes open, and it takes a few tries to get them to stay open. The room is dark, and there's a heavy weight on the side of my bed. I reach out, and my fingers slide over the top of Ivan's stubbled head.

He jerks up, and my hand falls away. "You're awake."

I stay still, keeping him in my sight like I'm afraid he'll disappear the second I glance off. "I guess I am. Or this is a very painful, very weird dream. What happened?"

"You got yourself shot. What the hell were you thinking?" His voice is a dark rumble of thunder.

The tone that usually rolls over me is inside me, but I'm numb and tingly right now. I glance up at the IV bag hanging over the bed. "I wasn't thinking. I just reacted. What did you see?"

Something crosses his face, and he swallows hard. "I wasn't paying attention to you or to Adrian. Not like I should have been. I was stalking your father. I killed him right before the assassin moved for Adrian. Apparently, she was waiting for someone to make a move on Arthur, and the second I touched him, she made her move as well."

I should feel sad about my father being dead, right? In this numb, tingly space, I don't care. Not one single bit about the man who abused me in the worst ways, and abandoned me at every turn, is gone. Another time, I might even be happy about it.

He drops his head, bracing it on my hand now. His forehead at the back of my palm. "I'm so sorry. I didn't mean to put you in more danger."

I scratch my fingers across his head. "You didn't put me in danger. My father did. He's always got to be one move ahead. I should have known he'd prepare something to try to ensure his own safety. He doesn't care about anyone but himself. I knew that too but didn't give you guys any kind of warning."

He stands and scoots onto the bed with me. It's a bed I don't recognize, with medical equipment surrounding the room on random steel trays. "Where are we?"

Ivan snuggles to my side and adjusts my pillow so I'm closer to him. "In the penthouse. Adrian wouldn't allow you to be taken anywhere else. The doctor showed up right after, and you had to be taken to the hospital for surgery. Everything seems to be going well, but you stayed asleep for a week, and it was the longest week of my life. Don't fucking do that to me again."

I'd laugh, but it would hurt. "I promise, I'll try not to get murdered saving your boss again."

There's a softness that comes across his features. "He's not just my boss, but my friend. We are a family. You didn't save my friend. You saved my brother. A man I respect more than anyone else in the world."

For him, it's a long speech. I'm mesmerized by his deep voice speaking each word. It has to be whatever painkillers they have me on, making me loopy as hell. "So what happened to Val? Did they get her out in time? Are she and the baby safe?"

"They are fine. Kai got them out the second he saw fast movement around Adrian. While he's glad she's safe, he regrets leaving Adrian's side. He considers himself Adrian's main protector. He might be second in the five, but he refuses to allow Adrian any leeway regarding his safety. He's upset that something like this happened, even though we knew it might."

Speak of the devil. I stare over the edge of the bed to watch Adrian walk into the room. He seems as calm and collected as he usually does.

"How are you feeling?"

I shrug, but it hurts too much to actually raise my shoulders. "Like someone shot me. Is everyone okay out there? Val? The baby?" Ivan just told me, but I'd feel better hearing it from Adrian or maybe Val herself. Not that I want her to see me like this. She's probably way more stressed than she should be right now.

Adrian steps closer, staring over Ivan's prone form. "Everyone is fine. Well, except you and your father. He's dead, by the way."

I nod. "I'll probably care more, one way or the other, once I get the hell off these meds."

"I owe you my life. Why would you step into a line of fire like that?"

With a long sigh, I close my eyes. "You both need to stop asking me that. You'd do the same for me in a heartbeat. Why is me sacrificing myself for you any different?"

Adrian places his hand on Ivan's arm. "Because he can't live without you."

I pop my eyes open, but Adrian is already walking out. I stare down at Ivan. "What did he just say?"

"He said I can't live without you, and he's right. This week has been the longest, most hellish week of my entire life. I don't want to live without you, Priscilla."

"I..." But words fail me at his declaration. I can hear the desperation in his tone, and it melts me from the inside out.

Gently, I wrap my hand around his cheek. "If I weren't laid out with a bullet wound right now, I'd be doing obscenely dirty things to you."

He smiles, and it knocks the breath out of me. "We can save it for when you're feeling better. It shouldn't take you long to recover. They did the surgery, but the bullet went straight through. They just had to make sure you were all closed up."

The thought of being opened up in some hospital makes me queasy, taking some of the shine off the moment. "So what happens now?"

"You recover, we go back to our lives, minus your asshole father, and live happily ever after."

I stare into his eyes and shake my head. "I don't believe in happily ever afters. It's a fairy tale, not real life."

He slides closer and tucks me against his side. "Then I guess I need to change your mind. If we are in a fairy tale, it's one of those fucked-up ones, but even then, it's going to have the ending we want."

I close my eyes and drift off, his voice in my head warming me, healing me in ways he doesn't even realize.

When I wake again, he's still there. The room is quiet and dark, the blinds drawn. I gently prod at my wound, and pain spears through me. "Shit."

He startles next to me and scrambles off the bed. "What do you need? Are you okay?"

I nod. "Fine. I gotta get used to the pain. I can't take the pain meds until it's completely gone."

His gaze narrows. "You sure as shit can. Right now, you could ask Adrian for the moon, and he'd bring it to you on a silver platter."

"It's the drugs. I don't like things in my body like that. Not after everything my father did, all the experiments."

Slowly, he climbs back into the bed and curls on his side next to me. No doubt so he can keep a close watch on every facial expression I make, hunting for any hint of pain. "You know I love you, right? I wanted to tell you so many times, but I didn't feel like I could. That I hadn't earned the right to say the words to you when your father still lived."

My heart tips in my chest, sending liquid warmth through my system. I feel like I've landed on a cloud, and my tattooed barbarian is the one holding it up in the sky. "What did you say?"

"You are my entire world, Priscilla. You calm the beast in me and make me want to be a better person. Well, you make me a better person on your own. If people need to die, I'm still going to kill them, but I'll listen to your opinion about it first."

There's a solemnity to his voice that touches me. I try to roll to my side, but it hurts, so I pull his face up to mine. "I love you too. More than anything in the world. I can't believe I get to keep you. That you're mine."

His mouth ticks up, full and beautiful, and makes me want to kiss him. "You do get to keep me because if you try to walk away, you won't get very far, I promise you."

I drift in and out for a while, bolstered by his presence and his words. The next time I wake, Val is with me, and Ivan is asleep in a nearby chair.

Val hefts herself out of the chair to stare at me in the bed. "How are you feeling?"

I give her the same answer I gave her husband. "Like I've been shot. Strangely, I'm happy, though."

She chuckles, then groans. "I only snuck in once he'd passed out. I needed to say thank you as well. I didn't want my child to grow up without a father."

I nod, uncomfortable with her thanks. "What happened to the woman who shot me, who tried to kill him?"

There's something she doesn't want to tell me. Her eyes drop to her feet, and she fists the covers as she maintains her precarious balance. "She's with Alexei right now. He's going to get the information we need."

"Will he torture her?"

She meets my eyes again. "Probably. But don't worry about it. Focus on getting better. On being with Ivan the way you deserve."

"How can I focus on that when she's being tortured. Can you let her go? Maybe she made a terrible mistake and needs the chance to fix it?"

Val grabs my hand and holds it between both of her own. "You might be right. She might get the chance, but that's not something you need to worry about. Get better. Focus on healing."

Ivan wakes and shoos Valentina out the door. When he takes me in his arms again, I sigh, letting myself relax, breathing him in. My entire world. My life. My husband.

Up next in this series is Bound to Punish

ABOUT THE AUTHORS

J.L. Beck is a *USA Today* and international bestselling author who writes contemporary and dark romance. She is also one half of the author duo Beck & Hallman. Check out her Website to order Signed Paperbacks and special swag.

www.bleedingheartromance.com

∼

Monica Corwin is a New York Times and USA Today Bestselling author. She is an outspoken writer attempting to make romance accessible to everyone, no matter their preferences. As a Northern Ohioian, Monica enjoys snow drifts, three seasons of weather, and a dislike of Michigan football. Monica owns more books about King Arthur than should be strictly necessary. Also typewriters...lots and lots of typewriters.

You can find her on Facebook, Instagram and Twitter or check out her website.

www.monicacorwin.com